Fool's Notion

Fool's Notion

Lisa J. Flickinger

Fool's Notion

Written by: Lisa J. Flickinger

ISBN: 978-1-7751297-0-7
Published by: Forget Me Not Romances, a division of Winged Publications
Cover design and page layout by: Cynthia Hickey

Scripture quotations are taken from The King James Version, The Authorized Version.

For Aurelia Ruby and Vienna Pearl, who blessed us by joining our family

Acknowledgements

A thank you goes out to Sybil and Carl Sewel of Windy Ridge Farms for the cups of tea and for sharing their love and understanding of four-legged friends.

Thanks also go out to Jodi for invoking the character of our hero by providing the name Cordell Sweet.

I also want to express gratitude to those women who left their homes behind to seek a new life out West and shared a wealth of knowledge through their diaries.

Chapter One

1883 California Trail, Kansas

Alda tucked her elbow into Bessie's flank and jabbed. "Bessie, if you don't get a move on soon, I'll whoop ya until …" Until what? Until nothing. Alda and the mule both knew the threat was emptier than a rusted-out tin pail. They hadn't moved an inch in over an hour.

Pushing auburn curls up into her bonnet, Alda turned and rested her back against the mule. The relentless Kansas sun brought rivulets of sweat to her forehead in place of the curls. She slid down the mule's back leg, landing with a soft *whump* on the dusty ground. Smoothing the green calico of her dress across her lap, Alda stared out across the tufts of thick, prairie grass. A small, brown lizard skittered up to her boot and then disappeared under a bleached stick.

"Fool's notion," Mamma had said, no more than a week before. And maybe she'd been right — God rest her soul. Why would a woman Alda's age, with no experience, attempt to drive the most stubborn animals ever created halfway across the country?

A low cough broke into her thoughts.

Alda jumped up, dusted her backside off and scrutinized the man smiling at her across Bessie's back.

"Ma'am." He tipped his black Stetson her direction. Dark chestnut waves dusted the top of his shoulders and a two-inch scar followed the curve of his right jaw.

Was the warm twinkle in his eyes on her account? Alda squared her shoulders and straightened her back.

"Could you use some help?" the stranger asked as he wrapped the reins of his mount around the saddle horn.

"I'll be fine, thank you. I wouldn't want to hold you up, Sir." Nor was she going to admit to needing assistance.

He swung a leg over and jumped to the ground. "I'm in no particular hurry."

"Bessie here's taking a break. We'll be moving along shortly." Alda slapped the mule on the hindquarter.

Bessie turned her head away from Alda, flipped her long ears, and stamped a hoof.

"If you don't mind me saying, Ma'am, I've been observing you for some time now."

Heat crept up her neck at the thought of him watching how little progress they'd made. Alda scanned the rolling prairie. She hadn't heard the cowboy or seen him until now. Pa would be madder than a hornet if he knew how careless she'd become. There was no escaping it, Pa was going to be madder than a hornet, regardless.

Alda brought her gaze back to the cowboy's. "My mule's fine. She's looking out for the others and figures they need a rest."

The lean cowboy stepped around Bessie and reached out his hand. "The name's Cord." His tanned, rough hand engulfed her tiny, white one. She remembered the blisters spread across her palm and withdrew it quickly. "Miss Alda Lealand. A pleasure to meet you, Mr. Cord."

"Cord will do, Miss, I'm not much into formality."

Alda turned the corners of her mouth up into what she hoped was a polite smile but not a welcome. If the fellow went on his way, she could show Bessie who was boss and get the pack string moving. The other mules had been patient so far, only eyeing up the lush prairie grasses along the road. She could have a mutiny on her hands before long.

Alda pinched her nose with her fingers, hunched over, and coughed as the air filled with a pungent aroma. "Bessie," she spluttered, "I swear you're trying to put me under like Mamma." As Alda backed away from the mule, she caught the smirk on Cord's face. He could think whatever he wanted. Much more of Bessie's flatulence and Pa would be planning Alda's funeral, too — if he could find her.

Cord stepped forward and scratched Bessie between the ears. "You suffering from colic, girl?" he asked, his voice low and soft as velvet.

Bessie dropped her head and closed her eyes. Her lips nibbled at the hem of his vest.

"Was your mule feeling poorly at sunup?"

How had he known she was on the road first thing this morning? She could have ridden out from nearby Scott Springs. "How long did you say you'd been watching my progress?" Alda took two steps and pulled Bessie's reins from the stranger's hands.

"I didn't," Cord said.

"Didn't what?"

"Didn't say, but I did ask if your mule was feeling poorly this morning."

Cord crossed his arms and leaned forward, forcing Alda to tip her head up to search his dark eyes.

"At first light she was, but not since we've been on the trail."

"You've been pushing her to mind, haven't you?"

Of course Alda had been pushing Bessie to mind, fifteen hundred miles was a long way to go. Bessie had hung her head and avoided the others at daybreak, and she'd been reluctant to start out on the trail. The further they'd gone, the more stubborn she'd become. Alda figured the mule was upset about leaving home.

"Let's go, Bessie. It's time you listen." Alda let the smooth leather slide through her hand in an attempt to pull the mule forward and force Cord to step out of the way.

He shifted his weight to the outside foot, his hand resting on Bessie's forehead, blocking Alda's path. "Your mule's in pain. I suspect colic. If you have any mineral oil, I'll see what I can do."

"Why colic? She hasn't been into any grain, and I didn't water the mules while they were hot." Pa loved his mules like family. Alda had spent half her life at his side, caring for them and training them. She knew how to avoid colic.

"Sometimes the mules get too much sand when they're grazing."

Alda looked out over the grass along the trail. The soil had been sandy the night before when she'd hobbled the animals. They grew fields of timothy back home — no sand for miles. How could Bessie know any better? How could Alda?

She let out a slow breath. "I've got mineral oil. Give me a couple of minutes." Alda wandered a few paces from the string and turned to eye the animals' packs. The mules weren't heaped up, as she didn't need a whole lot when traveling alone. But leaving the way Alda did, it was hard to remember what was packed where. One quick plucking from the medicine cabinet, and she'd filled a third of a flour sack. She remembered throwing something else in the sack to keep the bottles from knocking against one another and breaking, but what was it? Maybe the flour sack was in Old Joe's pack.

Alda crossed to the fourth mule in the pack string and loosened the rope tying the bundle together. She reached under the canvas cover to feel for the soft bulge of the flour sack. Her fingers touched solid bags of flour, rice, and cornmeal. It looked like Old Joe carried most of the dried food stores. She'd been more organized than she thought. Alda shifted the canvas back over the bundles and secured the rope. Where had she put that sack?

Cord scratched Bessie's withers. Alda couldn't hear the words he crooned to the mule, but judging by Bessie's relaxed hind leg and her floppy lower lip, the mule had forgotten her pain.

"Sure you don't need to be somewhere? If you tell me what to do with the oil, I'll look after the mule myself."

Cord lifted his head slowly; his direct stare bore right through her. "It's no job for a girl — alone."

Alda's nostrils flared and her small fists clenched at her sides. "Mister, I think it's about time you moved on."

"Like I said, the name's Cord, and this mule shouldn't have to suffer because you're too stubborn to let me help."

Mamma, I can't help it. "Mister, if I don't see your back riding away from here in the next ten seconds, I'm going to take my pa's rifle and shoot a hole through your middle so big the sun will shine right through it."

For a brief moment Cord's eyes widened and then he laughed — deep laughter that rolled from his belly. He leaned forward, putting his hands on his knees, to catch his breath.

Bessie opened her eyes and pricked her ears.

Alda grit her teeth and opened her mouth to lambaste Cord again when she noticed her father's rifle within Cord's reach and tied to her saddle.

Cord stood up and wiped the tears from his eyes. "Give me a moment, I'll have the rifle to you shortly, and then you can blast away." Cord pulled at one of the leather thongs securing pa's rifle.

Alda knew when to back down. Her temper had gotten the best of her, again, and she'd spoken before thinking. Ma had to remind her daily to *manage herself*. "Thanks, but I won't be needing my rifle." Alda nodded her head toward the mule string. "I'll take another look for that mineral oil."

"You mind if I remove her bridle and put her halter on while you're busy?"

Alda shrugged her response.

Cord's chuckle followed her progress as she rotated on one foot in the dirt and marched over to check another mule's pack.

Close to twenty minutes later, Alda located the sack with the medicine cabinet's contents in Jeremiah's pack and plunked it on the road. She unwound the twine from the top and reached in to remove a piece of rolled cloth. Two pairs of Mamma's drawers tumbled out onto the ground — stark white against the dirt brown. Pa had asked Alda to have her mamma's things sorted and given away before he returned from Excelsior Springs, where he'd gone five days before. When he informed her he was leaving, he said he'd been feeling poorly since her ma had died and figured the healing waters of the springs might cure what ailed him. Apparently taking care of the farm, on her own, was supposed to cure what ailed Alda.

She had put the under things in neatly folded stacks on the bed. When the idea struck her to head out before her pa returned, she'd thought the drawers made perfect wrapping for the assortment of multi-colored bottles. Right now, the idea was turning out to be a poor one. Alda snatched the drawers from the ground and stuffed them back into the worn sack.

"They're not mine," she said without turning to see if Cord had noticed or not.

"You fixing to open a store?"

So he had noticed. Alda didn't think the comment deserved a reply. She stalked out across the prairie to fish through her mother's unmentionables and find the mineral oil. A few minutes later, she returned and handed the bottle over to Cord. He removed the cork and handed it back to Alda along with Bessie's lead.

"I'll get her into position, and then you can give her the oil." Cord hooked a finger in the side of Bessie's mouth and wrapped an arm around her neck anchoring his shoulder under her throat.

Bessie twisted her neck in an attempt to pull herself form Cord's hold. Realizing it was hopeless, the mule pulled back on the lead and shifted her hind legs to find traction.

Alda tightened her grip on the rope and planted both feet in the sand to counterbalance the mule. There was no way she could keep Bessie from running off and pour the oil down her open throat at the same time.

"Pour it in slow; we don't want her breathing it in." Cord said.

Judging by the bulging veins along the man's neck, Cord was having a hard time trying to keep the mule in place.

"I can't." Alda sucked a breath of air into her lungs. "If I relax my grip, Bessie will hightail it out of here."

"Hold her tight then."

Hold her tight? Alda was giving Bessie's rope all she had.

Cord slipped his right hand from Bessie's mouth. The mule tried to shift her head toward Alda. Alda brought her shoulder to Bessie's jaw, coming within four inches of Cord's face. Sweat poured from under the brim of his black Stetson and coursed down his face making clean tracks that disappeared into the collar of his checked shirt.

His eyelashes were long and smoky, curling up at the ends — the kind a woman would die for.

"The oil," Cord grunted.

Right. Alda shifted the amber bottle from her fingers to Cord's while keeping a tight hold on Bessie's rope.

As Cord poured the mineral oil down Bessie's throat, she gurgled and gulped like a dying animal, splashing globules of the slippery liquid on both Alda and Cord.

"Let go!" he said as the bottle emptied, and he stepped back quickly.

Alda released the rope and tried to move out of Bessie's way. Not fast enough — Bessie's shoulder clipped her, and

Alda fell back on her bottom.

The mule shot a few yards from Alda and Cord, shaking her head trying to remove the foul taste of the mineral oil from her throat. When Bessie turned, she stood and eyeballed them — insulted they would subject her to such a practice.

Cord extended his hand. "Sorry about that," he said.

Alda reached up and took the offered hand. "No one's sorrier than I am."

Cord pulled her to her feet like she was nothing but feathers.

"I wish I'd known Bessie was in pain. How long do you think it will be before she gets some relief?"

Cord cleared his throat.

Alda looked down and realized she was still clutching Cord's hand. She dropped it, took a couple of steps back, and then she reached up to tuck a stray curl under her bonnet. No Bonnet. She brought both hands to the top of her head in an attempt to tame the riot of red curls she preferred to keep hidden.

"Looking for this?" Cord bent over to retrieve her bonnet from the ground at her feet. He swiped at it a couple of times then shook it, the pea green ties flapped in the wind.

She dropped her chin to her chest and waited for an inevitable comment like, *That explains the temper*, or *I can see now why you're so feisty*. Neither would be the worst comment of all, *Where'd all that red hair come from? You or your wife don't have red hair.* Like her ma was some woman of ill repute, or maybe her parents had found their daughter under a tree. Of course, Cord wouldn't say as much. He'd never met Pa, and he would never know her ma.

"You gonna take it?"

Alda looked down at the bonnet he'd thrust in her vision and then lifted her eyes for a quick glance. That's it?

No rude comments?

Cord pushed the bonnet at her again, and she reached out to grab it. She popped it on her head and deftly tucked her curls from view. "So how long, do you think, before Bessie starts feeling better?"

"You'll have to get her walking to move the oil through her system; she should be feeling a whole lot better by morning. I suggest you don't ride her anymore today. Alcove Springs is about fifteen miles up the way. It's a good spot to overnight, plenty of fresh water and good feed." He turned back to meet her eye. "But I suppose that's where you're headed. It's where a lot of folks on the trail spend the night."

Alda had heard the name before, but she hadn't paid any attention. Right now it was just one of the many small dots on her map, the map guiding her to Death Valley, California. "Yes, I plan to overnight at the springs and head out in the early morning." He didn't have to know she had made the plan while he was speaking; it was still a plan. "What makes you think I'm on the trail?"

Cord looked over at the string. "It doesn't appear that you're on a day trip. The size of your packs would indicate you either plan to get a fair way from here or you're in the supply business."

He was right. Although the packs weren't heaped, it was easy to tell she was going for more than a few days.

He gave her a lopsided grin. "So how far are you intending to go? It's a lot of responsibility, a full mule string, for someone your age and — "

Alda put her hands on her hips. "Gender? Granted mule skinners aren't typically women, but don't hold that against me. Under normal circumstances, these mules will mind."

"Typically? I've never met a female mule skinner before; you're nowhere near the type."

"What do you mean, nowhere near the type?"

"Loners who haven't bathed in weeks, men who can let

loose with a string of language so colorful, it's like they're painting a rainbow."

"Then I must come as a welcome surprise." Alda realized as soon as she said the words they sounded like she was fishing for a compliment. The sooner the cowboy moved on, the better. "What I mean to say is, I wish you well on your travels, Mr. Cord, and I thank you kindly for your help."

Cord arched an eyebrow and rubbed at the stubble on his chin. "I'll be taking my leave then. I have some business to attend to. If all goes well, I'll be seeing you in the morning."

"In the morning?" Would the man not leave her alone?

"I'd like to make sure Bessie here is all right, but I'll be arriving late tonight. I won't disturb you."

Of course, the mule. Alda's conscience jerked with the thought of the pain she'd caused the animal. "You'll be welcome at my campfire in the morning."

A broad smile creased Cord's face, lighting up his rugged features. "I look forward to it."

Why did the man cause her to say such things? Mamma would have been shocked. "Wh- what I meant was, I'd like to return the favor of your help with a hot breakfast if you are so inclined."

"I look forward to it even more, then. You have a good day." Cord tipped his hat and walked over to his mount, waiting patiently several paces away. He put a leather boot in the stirrup and slung his leg over the saddle.

Alda's, "You too," was lost in the wind at his back as he galloped across the prairie.

She watered the animals from the barrels Gideon carried. Since Moses was the only other mule broke to ride, she shifted his pack so he could lead the others to the springs. When they were on the move again, Bessie didn't look any worse for having to ingest the mineral oil and seemed content enough to follow the tail end of the string.

Alda walked for a few miles to stretch out the tight knots in her legs and back. It might be a while before she got used to the long days in the saddle.

The wind brought little relief from the sun's heat, and her lips felt dry and chapped. Alda brushed the back of her hand across them as she thought about the handsome cowboy who'd come to her rescue. A couple of wagons had passed while she'd been fighting with Bessie, but they'd moved along after a polite greeting, most likely because she'd refused to admit she needed help. It was a good thing Cord hadn't taken her *I'll be fine, thank you* for an answer, or Bessie might still be suffering.

Chapter Two

Cord would have to push his ride if he wanted to finish his business in Marysville and be over to Alcove Springs later tonight. "Get a move on, Boss; break's over." He nudged the grey gelding with the edge of his spurs, and the horse broke into a gallop. "We've got some miles to cover. The oats will be on me when we reach town, I promise."

He'd been on the trail too long. The first indication was talking to his horse. "Sorry, Boss. You're good company, but I'm afraid one of these days you're going to answer back, and then they'll be putting me away — maybe you, too."

Spending a half day in town would ease some of the loneliness, and so would tomorrow's visit with the spitfire he'd met that morning. He pictured Alda's curls when her bonnet had fallen to the ground. He'd never seen a head of hair quite so fascinating — the color of a new penny and just as shiny. He'd wanted to reach out and wrap one of those runaway curls around his finger. No telling what she might have done if he'd tried it. He smiled at the memory of her empty threat with her pa's rifle. He'd have to see if he could do something about that situation when he was in town today.

It was foolishness for a slip of a girl to be leading a pack string on her own. Not many folks used the old trails anymore, and a lot of those who did were up to no good.

She never did say how far she aimed to go. Maybe he could get her talking over the campfire in the morning and see what her plans were. The invitation to breakfast had come as a welcome surprise.

The sun was straight overhead when Cord rode onto the dusty Broadway Street. Lettered signs on the false fronted shops announced cabinets, blacksmith, furniture, and drugstore. Horses tied to hitching rails waited patiently outside the clapboard or brick buildings. They'd improved the place since his last visit by planting trees and shrubs in a makeshift boulevard.

He rode to the end of the street, reigned Boss to a stop in front of the Marysville Livery Stable, and dismounted.

A young boy in bare feet, with a straw tucked between his two front teeth, ran out of the double doors of the low roofed, stone building. Hitching up his trousers, he asked, "You looking to overnight your horse, Mister? My pa stepped out, but I'd be happy to help you."

"I'm in town for a few hours, but I promised Boss here some oats. If you wouldn't mind giving him a good rub down as well, it would be much appreciated." Cord loosed the cinch from the saddle, pulled it from Boss's back, and placed it on a tree inside the barn door.

"I'll take good care of him," the boy said as he picked up Boss's reins and led him toward a stall.

Cord sauntered down the plank sidewalk and turned the corner to the Sheriff's Office. A rusty hinge on the heavy metal door squeaked the notice of his arrival to the sheriff and two deputies jawing and drinking coffee in the front office.

"Well, if it ain't the mysterious Mr. Cord himself," Sheriff Richards said as he twisted the waxed corner of his expansive handlebar mustache and adjusted the badge pinned to the leather vest covering his hefty frame.

Sunshine from a small barred window cast stripes on the sheriff's face.

"I see you're working as hard as usual, Sheriff."

The sheriff's phlegmy chuckle turned into a coughing fit that nearly shook the building. The whip-thin deputy on his right pounded the sheriff's back as he leaned forward on the desk until the hacking subsided and he raised his palm. The sheriff wiped his mouth on the back of his hand and then wiped it on his pants before speaking. "Now why would I have to work hard when we have fine men such as yourself to do the work for us?"

Cord couldn't help the smile spreading across his face and creasing the corner of his eyes. It was the same banter they always tossed. "Now, Sheriff, I'm quite certain I don't know what you are referring to."

"Deputies, if you would please excuse us."

The whip and his cohort scooted around the desk and disappeared through the door leading to the jail cells across the back of the building.

Sheriff Richards opened a drawer, withdrew a wad of folded bills, and tossed them onto the center of the desk. "I assume you're here to collect these."

Cord reached out to retrieve the cash.

The sheriff stuck a beefy, pointer finger on the wad and pressed. "Not so fast, Mr. Preston Cordell Sweet."

Cord clamped his jaw. The vein in his neck pulsed as he cracked three of the knuckles on his left hand one by one. "Who've you been talking to?" Cord asked, his voice a low growl.

"Don't be angry with me, son. I didn't go looking for answers. Have a seat."

Cord exhaled the breath he'd been holding and sat down on one of the worn oak chairs in front of the desk.

"Is there a good reason you don't want your family to know your whereabouts? The fellow who came round said they were genuinely concerned about you."

Cord looked the sheriff straight on and steeled himself so he wouldn't show any reaction. Richards was good at reading people; there was a reason the man was sheriff, even though he could barely cross the room on his own steam. "Who came round, and when?"

"Short fellow, finely dressed, bit of an English accent; he showed up a couple of days ago and showed me a picture of a man in full military dress. I must say, you clean up well." The beginnings of a laugh rumbled through the man's chest. The sheriff avoided another coughing fit as he calmed himself and cleared his throat.

Cord rubbed the three days' worth of growth on his chin. Hayden was looking for him? "Why here, in Marysville?"

"Not just here. The fellow's been to several towns in the area."

Cord knew it wouldn't last, the freedom he'd felt when his father said he didn't want to ever see or hear from him again. His mother must have won him over, and now Hayden was searching him out for the family. Why couldn't they leave him alone? Now, because of their meddling, they might have destroyed his livelihood. "Is this going to compromise our arrangement?"

"Depends," Sheriff Richards said, "on whether you tell me why they're looking or not. You got a wife and family you're not supporting? Did you abscond with the family fortune?"

Cord smirked. If his mother had had her way, there would have been a daughter-in-law and a couple of children; but she hadn't, and she wasn't going to either.

And would he be on the trail day after day if he had the family money? Nope. His father saw to it that Cord walked away without a cent. No prodigal son generosity ran in that man's bones.

"To answer your questions, no and no."

Sheriff Richards raised a bushy eyebrow. "That's all you got for me — no?"

"The job depends on anonymity, doesn't it?" It wasn't

likely Cord could stall much longer. Richards had a reputation for thorough interrogation.

"I know what you look like. I now know your full name and your family. You're not anonymous to me. Talk."

"What's to say? My family was looking for their fourth-generation professional soldier. They laid my whole life out for me—who I would fight, where I would live, who I would marry. But I don't fit the mold."

"I can see that."

"I like riding, I like wide open spaces, and I like to think I'm helping people." People like cute little redheads having trouble with their mules. Cord raised his eyes to the sheriff's. "People like yourself, Sheriff."

"I can live with that, Preston, if you tell me for sure you're on the up and up."

"It's Cord, Sir, and I'm clean. Did you tell the man anything?"

"No, son, your secret's still safe with me." The sheriff leaned over and slid the cash toward Cord.

Cord picked it up and stashed it in his pocket.

"That's for that varmint Toad you brought in. He was a slippery fellow, almost snuck out the back door when we weren't looking."

"Might have worked in my favor. The price goes up, doesn't it, if the criminal escapes again?"

The sheriff smiled and pointed his finger. "Don't you go thinking that way, or you will end up on the wrong side of the law."

"So you got anything else for me?"

The sheriff opened another drawer, rifled through some papers, and dropped a wanted poster on the desk. The poster pictured a medium build, disheveled man wearing a battered cowboy hat and with a belt full of ammunition across his chest. On either side, two young men sporting fancy, beaded, leather vests held their pistols aloft like they were in a Wild West show. The wording across the bottom said, "Wanted, Dead or Alive, Doc Rufus and sons Owen and Emmett also known as the Doc Rufus gang. For train robberies committed in Wyoming, Nebraska, and Kansas. Reward of $1,000 for Doc Rufus and $500 each for sons Owen and Emmet."

"They've been shooting up Indians for sport, too. Hard to say who will find them first."

Cord took another glance at the picture. "I'm hoping it's me."

"It will go better for them if that's true. The Indians don't take kindly to white folks killing their braves for no reason and then wearing the trophies. Be careful. These guys are ruthless killers. They don't seem to have any problem shooting anybody between them and their take. Last time out, they shot a couple of women who wouldn't hand over their rings on the train."

Cord folded the poster into a square he could fit in his pocket. "Anyone else?"

"A petty thief named Felix. He's been stealing trinkets from folks along the California Trail—watches, lockets, shiny stuff and not all of it valuable. He hasn't been seen much. People have been complaining about missing items accompanied by a terrible stench."

"Now that's one I haven't heard before."

"Me neither. Apparently the man needs to take a bath. Don't think he's much of a danger, but you never can tell. The bounty's only $100.00. It should be easy enough. The fellow's been sniffed, I guess you could say, in the area."

Cord stood up from his chair and stuffed the wanted poster with the cash in his pocket. "Thank you, Sheriff. I'll be taking my leave now. I've got a bit of business in town."

"What kind of business?"

What did it matter what kind of business?

"Just some business."

"You've never done your business in town before. Why now?"

"How would you know, Sheriff?"

"I know everything that goes on in this town. Particularly, if the best bounty hunter I got decides to stick around."

"I'm looking for some fancy, leather work."

"Fancy, leather work? Like a vest or something?"

Heat built up inside Cord's collar. "I was thinking of a scabbard for a shot gun, maybe some decorative tooling on it."

"If I were to guess by the color creeping up your neck, I would say you were thinking of having flowers or hearts put in the design."

Cord twisted on his heel and stalked to the door.

"Ask for Benny at the general store and tell him I sent you. He'll get you fixed up with something purty," the sheriff said to Cord's back.

Cord lifted his hand in a backward wave. "Don't work too hard, Sheriff."

"You know I won't."

Cord left the building and walked back toward Broadway. It was true. He had never spent time in Marysville once his business with the sheriff was done. He hadn't spent much time anywhere for that matter. There was always the next bad guy to track down. The thrill of the chase often meant he didn't sleep or eat much for days on end.

He stopped to ask a fellow in front of the barber shop where a man could get a good meal and was directed to a one story, brick building across the street. Cord filled himself to the brim with broiled mutton chops, potatoes and gravy, and then topped it off with a large slice of pound cake and a steaming mug of coffee. He would've liked to follow the meal up with a long nap.

After paying his bill and generously tipping the worn out waitress who served him, Cord sauntered to the General Store three doors down. A slight fellow with gold, wire rimmed glasses and a white apron tied around his waist stood behind the room length counter, wrapping a parcel in brown paper.

He glanced up as Cord entered. "Can I help you?"

"The sheriff said you might have some leather work for sale. He said to ask for Benny."

"That's me." The fellow pushed his spectacles up with a pointer finger and resumed tying a piece of twine around the square package. "Anything in particular you're looking for?"

"A scabbard for a shot gun, and I was hoping it might have some tooling on it." Cord shifted the weight to his outside foot and dried the palms of his hands on his jeans. "And maybe I could have a name added."

"I've got a couple in the back," Benny said before scurrying through a cloth door behind him. When he returned, he laid two leather scabbards on the counter. The first was a glossy black with a rope design following the edge and a shiny buckle in the middle. The second was a burnished brown with scroll work at both ends and a short fringe hanging from the bottom.

Cord ran his hand the length of the second. "Do you think you could add a name across the middle here?"

"The shop's been quiet today. Probably take about an hour, if you can wait that long."

"I can wait."

"All right, what name would you like me to add?"

Chapter Three

Late afternoon shadows brought Alda and the pack string to Alcove Springs, *a good spot* indeed. Blended shades of emerald and jade draped the trees surrounding the falls. Layered rock formed a half moon shelf about ten feet high, and a blanket of water cascaded into a shallow basin. A narrow scarf of moss grew along the rocks of the stream bubbling out from the basin.

The mules shifted on their hooves and eyed the stream.

"Looks like we have the place to ourselves." Alda pulled Moses's bridle over the mule's ears and removed the bit from his mouth. "At least until our knight in shining armor arrives."

The Mule dropped his head and nibbled at the heads of the knee-high grass growing in the meadow. Each of the other nine mules did the same as Alda removed their halters, unloaded their packs, and stacked them under a leafy maple tree. She watered the string at the stream before collecting the hobbles from Arthur's pack and hobbling the mules. She didn't want a repeat of the first night on the trail. Jenny and Bud had wandered off by morning, causing Alda to waste precious hours trying to catch the runaways on the vast prairie.

After pitching her canvas tent under the same maple, Alda pulled her tall, leather riding boots off and rubbed the balls of both feet. The last ten miles had been more walking than she was used to. She removed her cotton stockings and wriggled her toes before lifting the skirt of her dusty dress and wandering closer to the falls. Prairie clover tickled her knees, and the cool grass felt refreshing against the multiple blisters running along her toes.

Carved names and dates of other travelers marked the rocks near the water. Her finger traced the warm, deep grooves in a large stone. J F Reed, 26 May, 1846. *What brought you to leave your home, J F Reed, and take to the trail? Was it land or maybe gold — the promise of riches? Or were you trying, like me, to secure a different future for your family?*

Alda walked to the water's edge and knelt down. She lifted a scoop of the cool water; it stung her lips before slipping down her throat. She dipped again — thirsty for water that didn't carry the metallic taste of her canteen. She drank several more scoops before removing her bonnet and rinsing her face and neck.

The directness of Cord's gaze when she'd lost her bonnet rose in her memory. She was certain he would make a comment. He'd seen enough of her wild temper to make the same connection everyone else did. But why did people blame her disposition on the color of her hair? Whether her hair was black, blond, brown, *or red,* she'd be just as riled up when a man insinuated she was a mere girl. In four months, she would turn nineteen. Mamma had been married and with child by the time she turned eighteen. Alda was no girl. And what business was it of Cord's to decide what she could and couldn't do?

Maybe Alda had a few things to learn, but eventually colic would have occurred to her, too. With a little coaxing, Bessie would have taken the mineral oil from her. Cord wasn't the only person who knew animals. For all his faults, Pa had taught her well. He would be hopping mad when he found a string of his mules missing.

Alda opened the flap of her tent and tossed in her bedroll. With a few sticks and her flint, she built a fire in one of the soot blackened rings of rocks nearby. Using a small, cast iron pot suspended from a forged tripod, she fried up bits of bacon and chopped onion. After pouring a portion of the grease out, she added equal amounts of water and rice and let it simmer. The salty bacon made the rice tolerable, and it was easy to pack on the trail.

Alda ate her fill of the mixture and then crossed the field over to the stream and washed her cooking utensils. The previous two nights they'd received only a quick rub with sand. With a bit of lye soap, she washed her stockings and laid them out to dry on a branch.

The mules hadn't spread far and were either nibbling at the thick grasses or taking small drinks from the stream.

As darkness settled in, Alda climbed into the tent with a lantern to read by. She allowed herself one hour of lantern time each night. The kerosene had to last the entire journey, and she was too exhausted to read any longer anyway. If she could, she would trade her best mule for a feather bed and a pillow — any pillow. She'd used plenty of pillow cases for packing but had forgotten to pack a pillow. Her rolled up skirt wasn't comfortable. Alda pulled the worn copy of *The Adventures Tom Sawyer* out of her pack. Even the fourth time through, Tom's antics and wit made for interesting reading.

After snuffing the lantern, Alda closed her eyes and let her weary mind wander. She missed her Ma something terrible, but thinking about her opened up a dark hole, a hole so deep she was afraid if she entered the darkness she might never come back. Alda squeezed her eyes shut and rubbed her fists into them like she had since the day Ma died. There'd be plenty of time to mourn when she got back home.

And then she pictured Cord, his eyes when they'd first met hers. The bulge of his biceps as he'd held the mule's head still so she could administer the mineral oil. His pleased smile when she'd invited him for breakfast.

Knowing he would be nearby might help her to sleep better, too. After three nights of waking at every strange sound, she'd grown mighty tired. Her eyelids fluttered as she drifted off into slumber.

Alda startled and gripped the edge of her quilt. "Who's there?" She'd heard a distinct rub of metal on metal. Maybe it was only one of the mule's hobbles. Pulling the blanket up to her chin, she rolled onto her side and closed her eyes.

"Oomph."

Alda's eyes popped open. "Cord, is that you?" Her voice rose. "Cord?" She lifted the edge of the blanket and crawled quietly to the front tent flap. Using one finger to make a gap, she peered out into the darkness.

Her nose caught a whiff of something fierce, and she let the flap close to pinch her nostrils. Her stomach rolled. "Bessie, you not feeling well again?" Alda threw her shawl around her shoulders and crawled through the tent opening to go and see to her mule.

Standing upright, her breath hitched, and her hand flew to her chest.

A man as old as her father crouched beside the dying coals of her fire. He held her tin plate in one hand and her spoon in the other. He appeared to be the source of the awful stench —half outhouse, half vomit.

Alda swallowed.

"Ma'am, I don't mean you no harm." His slurred voice was high pitched — almost a squeak.

Alda swallowed again. The shot gun was with the packs under the tree. She slid one foot toward them and tightened the grip on her shawl.

The fellow wiped a grimy hand across each corner of his mouth, caught the bits of spittle, and then wiped them across his chest. "You mind if I take these?" He held the plate and spoon aloft.

Alda slid another step toward the rifle. "Are you hungry? I cleaned up my supper, but I can fetch some salt pork and dried fruit from my pack if you like … and send you on your way."

And collect her Pa's rifle while she was at it.

Where are you, Cord?

"I'm not particularly hungry. I had a good fill at the last farm. But I wouldn't mind relieving you of these."

Alda bit the edge of her lip. She could make a run for it, but the man might be packing a pistol. Stupid, mighty stupid leaving home alone; she should've waited until Pa returned and convinced him to come along. If he had refused, she could've found someone else.

The man's eyes seemed transfixed at her chest level. Alda looked down. Her ma's gold locket peeked out of the vee of her shawl. "Take the plate and spoon," she raised her voice, "and get out of here." Flinging her arm out for emphasis, she gained another step toward the packs.

"Now, Ma'am, I said I didn't mean you no harm, and I don't. But I'll be taking that pretty bauble you got hanging around your neck with me when I go."

Over her dead body, he'd be taking the pretty bauble. She pulled at the chain of the locket and tucked it inside the neck of her nightgown. She steadied her voice. "I said get out of here."

The fellow poked at the fire with a stick, and the coals brightened to a small flame. He didn't look up as he spoke. "You gonna give me that locket?"

"I can't. It was my ma's, and it's all I got left. My pa killed her, and we buried her last week."

The fellow's shoulder twitched as he nudged a coal. "I'd take good care of it for you. Polish it up. It couldn't have a better home."

Keep him talking, only four more steps to the rifle. "What are you talking about? A thief like you would unload it as soon as possible and probably go drink the money away soon after."

The man jumped up from the fire. "I'm no thief!" he

hollered and charged her.

Alda spun and dove for the rifle. The man landed on her back, forcing the air out of her chest. Stunned, Alda gulped for breath as the man tugged at her hair, searching for the chain. Grass and dirt dug into her cheek as the man crushed her face against the ground. Her chest heaved as her breath returned, and she tried to twist out from under him. Her nails scrabbled at the ground without gaining purchase. "Get off me!"

"Gimme that locket," he hissed in her ear.

The smell of his hot breath rivaled his body odor. Alda gagged.

A gun clicked, and the man stilled.

"Stand up slowly," Cord said. "You make one move I don't like, and this will be your last day on earth."

The man lifted his weight off Alda.

Alda sucked in a ragged breath, curled into a ball, and covered her face with her hands. Screams hurled out of her chest with a force all their own. "Mamma! — Mamma! — Maammaaaaaa."

Minutes or hours later, Alda had no idea, a hand touched her shoulder. She scrambled up from the ground and backed into the packs under the maple. Her hand sought out Pa's rifle, and she swung it around — cocking back the hammer.

Cord was perched, one knee in the grass, in front of her. "It's me, Alda. You're safe," he said, his voice low and calm. "Are you all right? Did he hurt you any?"

Alda shook her head.

Cord exhaled a long, slow breath. "I've cuffed the guy, Alda. Other than his smell, he won't be doing any more damage tonight."

Alda dropped the rifle and pulled her shawl from the grass. She rolled it up, placed it on her knees, and buried her face. Sobs wracked her shoulders. "He wanted my mamma's locket. My mamma loved her locket, and it's all I got left. I couldn't give him my mamma's locket … I just couldn't."

Cord patted her shoulder. "Shhh now. You're all right. He won't be taking your ma's locket." Cord's grip stilled on her shoulder. "I'll take him to the sheriff tomorrow, and he won't be taking anything from anybody for a good long while."

Alda lifted her face from her shawl. "Thank you. I don't know what would have happened if you hadn't —"

"You don't need to worry about that. The good Lord brought me here in time."

Alda swiped at her eyes with her sleeve. "The Lord doesn't pay me much mind."

Cord blinked. "I'm glad He did tonight. You climb into your tent and try and get some rest. I'll sit by the fire for a bit and keep an eye on things." He took his hat from his head and held it — running his fingers around the brim. "Felix is cuffed to a tree across the meadow. You're safe now."

"Felix? You know him?"

"I know *of* him."

"How?"

"It's late. We can talk in the morning. You owe me breakfast, remember?"

Alda searched Cord's eyes. He'd said the good Lord brought him. She didn't deserve it, but she was glad He did send Cord. "I remember. Wake me when you want to head out, and I'll make us some flapjacks and bacon."

Cord reached out and gave her shoulder one last squeeze. "Good night, Alda."

Alda waited until he sat down beside the fire before climbing into her tent. She brushed the grass and dirt from her nightgown and climbed back into her bedroll. Felix's hideous scent lingered on her skin, but she was too exhausted to do anything about it. She wrapped her arms around her shoulders to still their quaking. What would have happened if Cord hadn't shown up when he did? How far would Felix have gone to get the locket? Would he have stopped at taking the locket?

As Alda stared at the white canvas of her tent, she recalled her ma's kind eyes and sweet smile. They'd spent many a night together, when the day's work was done, sitting by the fire and swapping tales. Mamma was a wonderful storyteller. It wasn't fair that she'd been taken so young.

The last few months, it seemed like Ma had given up. She'd only shrugged when the doctor said he couldn't do any more for her. And she'd grown so thin, hardly the size of a child by the end. Alda's heart warmed thinking about the many family and friends who'd gathered by the grave up on the hill to honor her ma's life. With the cuffs of her cotton nightgown, she caught the overdue tears sliding from her eyes.

The sun was well up the horizon when Alda awoke the next morning. "Cord, you still here?"

"I'm still here. If I had known you were such a woman of leisure, I might not have agreed to have breakfast with you."

Kicking off her covers, she slid from the bedroll. Thank goodness the man had stuck around. "I guess being scared within an inch of my life took more out of me than I thought. I'll be with you shortly." Alda pulled her nightgown up over her head and dressed for the day. She eyed her green bonnet in the corner. The man had seen her flaming curls at their worst; might as well eat breakfast without it. She ran a comb through her hair and fastened it into a tight roll at the nape of her neck.

When Alda emerged from the tent, Cord sat by the fire like he'd never left it. Only the added firewood gave any indication he'd ever moved. The mules appeared content munching the grass in the meadow. Felix sat with his arms wrapped around a tree a few yards from the stream. Seeing him in the daylight made her stomach knot. "You said you'd tell me how you knew that varmint. I can still smell him from here."

"Morning, Alda." Cord said and tipped his hat.

"Good morning. Are you going to tell me or not?"

"Depends."

Alda put her hands on her hips. "Depends on what."

"How good your breakfast is."

Was that a smirk? Alda sniffed and walked over to dig through the packs for the vittles.

"I'll have you know, he would have smelled a whole lot worse if I hadn't wrangled him into the stream this morning. He put up quite a fuss. I'm surprised you could sleep through the racket."

"Am I expected to feed the scoundrel, too?"

Alda opened a leather pouch and sliced a chunk of bacon from a large slab. After she cut the chunk into thick slices, she tossed them in her cast iron frying pan and put them on the fire. Cord raised an eyebrow when she handed him a fork and asked him to watch the bacon. There was no reason he couldn't make himself useful.

Into a large tin bowl, she measured two cups of flour, a pinch of salt, and enough buttermilk to make a smooth batter. The farmer she'd given a couple of pennies to for buttermilk, the evening before, had lifted his worn hat and scratched his forehead when he'd seen her and the string of mules, but he hadn't asked any questions. It was just as well; she wouldn't have answered them anyway.

"It'd be the kindly thing to do, feeding Felix some breakfast," Cord said.

"I'm not feeling too kindly toward that man." She cracked one of her surviving eggs on the edge of the bowl and added it to the batter.

"I'm sorry he scared you, Alda. I wish I'd happened on him sooner. The man's not in his right mind. He said something this morning about your pa killing your ma. Is there any truth to that?"

Alda's hand stilled from stirring the batter. It had slipped out. The feeling she hadn't meant to speak. "I guess we both have secrets."

"At least until after breakfast."

Alda glanced over at Cord. He held her gaze until she looked away.

During breakfast, Alda moved bits of flapjack from one side of her plate to the other. The food was like a lead ball in her stomach. The previous night's events didn't appear to have affected Cord's appetite. He'd taken a heaping plate across the field to Felix and watched the man wolf it down before coming back for his second and third helping.

"You gonna eat that or just give it some exercise?" Cord held his plate out towards hers. "I could help you out, if you like."

Alda scraped the majority of her breakfast onto his plate. "I guess I'm not hungry. Is this when we talk? You must be happy enough with breakfast or you wouldn't be begging for my leftovers."

"It's a fine breakfast, and I thank you for it. What do you want to know?"

"You said yesterday you'd heard about Felix. How?"

"When I went to Marysville, I heard about a petty thief, known for his offensive smell. There was a reward out. I'll split it with you, seeing as you pretty much captured the man."

She could use the money, badly, but there was no way she could take it. "I don't find you particularly humorous this morning. Is that all he's known for, thieving? Did he ever hurt anybody?" Alda looked across the meadow at Felix dozing under the tree, and her spine tingled at its base.

"Nope. But there's always a first time."

Alda glanced over at Cord. "Are you giving me a warning?"

"Are you going to take one? It's not safe, you, out here on your own."

Alda shifted her hips and toed the dirt with her boot.

"And why are you traveling alone? Where's your family? Was Felix telling the truth? Did your pa kill your ma?"

"It's the truth as I see it. The doctor said cancer. I say she was worked to death by my pa."

"And how's that?" Cord asked.

"We're known for miles around for our mules. You can see for yourself they're top notch."

"Missouri mules, if I'm not mistaken."

"The best there is, but Pa's a dreamer, and he wouldn't sell them."

"What do you mean he wouldn't sell them?"

"Ever. We've been raising mules for nine years, and he never sold a single one. We've had some die on us, some of our best stock, but we never sold any. "

Cord pinched his bottom lip between his thumb and finger.

"It wasn't for lack of customers either, but you can only string people along for a while before they lose interest. We sold crops — the prices have been dropping for years. We sold land — down to our last two hundred acres, and we sold the family heirlooms — until there were none left. But Pa still wouldn't sell the mules."

Alda rubbed her mother's locket between her thumb and pointer finger. "My ma came from money. Her folks warned her not to marry my pa, but she went ahead anyway. Because of that, she said she would never take a cent from her folks. My pa would've. He probably would have taken everything they had."

Cord shook his head as he stirred up more flames in the coals.

"My mamma sold eggs, did other people's laundry, and we made preserves enough for the entire county, but it wasn't enough to keep so many animals fed. Ma always said the mules would eat us out of house and home, and they did just that."

"It makes no sense. Why not sell a mule or two?"

"I guess pa was a dreamer and a gambler. The price was always going up, and if he held out he'd make that much more. He hasn't paid the property taxes for three years, and now the county's sending letters of foreclosure. I don't want to lose the home place." Alda pictured the farm in her mind. "We're only a couple of miles from the river near Wayne City. My pa was never one to skimp. We've got a first rate barn, and four years ago Pa built my ma the two story house she always wanted. Her gardens were her pride and joy."

"Your pa doesn't know, does he?"

Was it that obvious? Alda dropped her chin to her chest. "Doesn't know what?"

"You're on your own with his mules."

Alda shrugged, and her voice dropped to a whisper. "No, he doesn't know, but it wasn't all my idea. My uncle came up with the offer, and I convinced my ma I could deliver the mules. She set it all up before she died. Pa took off two days after the funeral and didn't say a word about when he was coming back. Maybe my ma saw it coming, and it's why she agreed."

"So you're fixing to sell. I've heard mules are making a pretty penny in Nebraska."

"Yeah, I'm fixing to sell, but not in Nebraska."

"You going as far as Colorado?"

Alda swallowed and shifted her eyes to the dancing flames of the fire. "No, I'm not going to Colorado."

"Where to?"

"Death Valley, California."

"Death Valley? Are you out of your mind? That's clear across the country. There's no way you're gonna make it."

Alda clenched her fists in her lap and looked Cord in

the eye. "I'm going to make it; and when I do, I'm selling the string for the one hundred and twenty a piece they're offering, and then I'm saving our home. No one, not even you, can stop me."

"Girl, there's got to be any easier way. Why aren't you shipping the animals in a cattle car? You'd be saving weeks of hardship."

"Stop calling me girl."

A look of puzzlement crossed Cord's face at her outburst. "All right, Miss Alda, why aren't you shipping the animals?"

"I hardly have two pennies to rub together. I can't afford to ship them. But it's more than that. I need time. Time to do some thinking — time away from my pa — and two months ought to do it."

"It's not right."

"What's not right? Look here, if you're intending to give some sermon about stealing my pa's livestock, I don't — "

"To let you go. It's not right to let you go — "

"I'm not asking for your permission, and I'm not asking for your help either." The words tumbled from Alda's mouth. "Though I thank you for your assistance last night."

Cord's laugh held a harsh edge.

"I mean to go. I'm bringing the pack string to my Uncle Larkin. The deal's set for one thousand eighty dollars."

"Alone. It wouldn't be right to let you go, alone."

Alda's heart thumped a heavy beat in her chest. "You mean —"

"I don't know what I mean." Cord uncrossed his boots, stood by the fire, and placed his hands on his hips. "I'll be taking Felix to Marysville now."

Chapter Four

"Get a move on, you sorry creature." Cord whipped the backside of Felix's swayback appaloosa with his lariat, and the horse moved into a trot.

Felix bobbed and dipped, trying to keep his balance on the tattered saddle. "You trying to break my neck? You gotta undo these cuffs."

"Nope."

"Then I'm going to tell the sheriff you've been treating me with undue harshness. I know my rights."

Cord sniggered. "Well then, a smart guy like you should know that a bounty hunter like me does not have to uphold the due process of the law."

Felix whipped his head around; greasy, greying curls bounced across his brow. "Bounty hunter? There's a bounty out for me?" Felix straightened his shoulders and puffed out his chest as his horse slowed. "Do I got posters and everything?"

"No, you don't have any wanted posters out for you, you dolt." Cord reached out and encouraged Felix's mount back into a trot. "Stealing's not something to be proud of."

"Ouch. I was doing all right until I picked on your girl. I'll bet no one else even notices their stuff is gone, and I take good care of it."

"They notice Felix, and she's not my girl."

"Whadya mean she's not your girl? I see the way you look at her. I can tell. You're smitten."

Not likely, the girl had less sense than one of her mules. What was she thinking, heading out across the entire country by herself? It would have been better for him if he'd never come across her. But it was too late. He knew she was on the trail and that made him accountable, didn't it? Now he had to decide what he was going to do about it. The girl needed protection; that's for sure.

"Drat!"

"What's that?" Felix asked.

"Nothing. I forgot something, that's all."

"I know what you forgot, to undo my cuffs."

"A present, I forgot the present I picked up yesterday." Alda's new scabbard lay in his pack. In all the kerfuffle he'd forgotten to give it to her.

"A present for the girl — who's not your girl."

"Felix, you're getting on my nerves."

Broadway Street in Marysville bustled with Saturday business as Cord and Felix rode into town.

"You going to take these things off?" Felix raised his cuffed wrists in the air. "I look like a criminal"

"You are a criminal, and the sooner I drop you off the better. I can't take much more of your scent. What's with you and the lack of personal hygiene?"

"People don't tend to bother you when you smell like I do. It leaves me free to do my business."

"Thieving. You mean your thieving."

"I'm a collector, not a thief. I'll tell you what. You look through my pack here, and you can take anything you like. I won't fault you if it's some of my choice treasures. Then you and I can part ways; no need to get the sheriff involved."

"You got anything worth a hundred bucks?"

"I might have if you'd have let me take the pretty locket."

Cord gave Felix a dark look before stopping their horses in front of the Sheriff's Office. "You're something else, Felix." He dismounted and snugged their reins around the hitching post. After pulling Felix from his horse, Cord grabbed the man's upper arm and marched him up the front walk.

Four deputies stood round the desk. They turned and parted when Cord hauled Felix through the front door.

"Is the sheriff in?"

The heavyset deputy from the day before spoke first. "No he's not in, and he might not be for a good long while — maybe never."

Cord eyed the deputy, trying to decipher his meaning. "What are you saying, he might not be back?"

"Sheriff Richards' health took a turn for the worse. Murphy here," he nodded to his partner, "found him on the floor this morning. The doc thinks it might have been a heart attack. He said to send you over when you showed."

"So he's all right?"

"Probably not. He said you'd be back in the next day or two with the petty thief, and he
needed to talk to you. I'm assuming this foul smelling critter is him?"

The sheriff put too much faith in Cord's ability. If it hadn't been for Felix catching up with Alda, Cord probably wouldn't have caught him. Cord dug his finger into Felix's back harder than necessary to push him toward the deputies. "Yeah, this is him. Where would I find the sheriff?"

Felix lost his footing and tumbled to the floor. "There you go, more of that unnecessary harshness. You deputies see that?"

"Two streets over, the three story blue on the corner." The thin deputy said as he pulled Felix from the floor and shoved him through the door to the cells.

Cord jogged over to the sheriff's and rapped on the scroll worked, screen door. A tall woman with black hair pulled into a severe bun answered his knock.

"I'm here to speak to the sheriff. How's he doing?"

"The doctor just left." She drew in a long breath. "Unfortunately, he didn't hold out much hope for recovery. I told the deputies not to send anyone over." She raised a finely curved eyebrow. "May I ask who you might be?"

"Cord, Ma'am, you give the sheriff my best." Cord turned to leave. It wasn't right to disturb the sheriff even if he asked him too.

"One moment." The woman let the door close and disappeared inside. A minute later, she returned and opened the door for Cord to enter. "Percy would like to talk to you. Please keep it brief. He doesn't have much strength."

Cord followed the swish of the woman's skirts down the dimly lit hall to what looked like a formal parlor. The furniture was pushed back to line the walls and to accommodate the four-poster bed in the center of the room where the sheriff reclined on a mound of pillows. His face carried a greyish pallor. The man had aged twenty years overnight.

The sheriff cleared his throat weakly. "Cord, meet my wife, Belle."

Wife? The woman looked to be twenty years younger.

Belle turned and smiled, extending her hand as she did so. "So nice to meet you, Mr. Sweet."

Cord shook the woman's hand. What was the sheriff doing telling her his real name?

"I see your confusion, Cord. My wife knows all about you. In fact, my wife knows everything that goes on in my office. She provides a fresh perspective and keeps me from losing my mind. Don't worry; Belle won't talk, and the facts won't go any further." The sheriff wrapped his large hand around his wife's fingers. "A man couldn't ask for a better help mate."

Belle put her other hand on top of the sheriff's. A look of love, warm and intimate, passed between the two. Cord could feel the tips of his ears turning red. He stepped back and rubbed the back of his neck. "I shouldn't be disturbing you, Sheriff; I'll come back when you've regained your strength."

Belle released her husband's hand, and her quick fingers smoothed the folds of the patterned quilt across his lap. "Please stay. Percy's been meaning to talk to you for some time now." She flashed a quick smile in Cord's direction and then said, "Don't tire yourself out, Percy. I'll be in the kitchen if you need anything," and bustled out of the room.

"Have a seat, Cord," the sheriff said and pointed to the overstuffed chair by the bed.

Cord removed his hat and stuck it on his knee as he sat down. "What did your wife mean by you've wanted to talk to me for some time?"

"I should have talked to you sooner, when the Lord first laid you on my heart."

"The Lord?"

"You a believer, son?"

Cord shifted in his seat. "Yes, Sir, I'm a believer. I'm not sure what that has to do with me and you, Sheriff."

"You're the best bounty hunter I got. I can see your eyes fire up when I tell you about what some of these men have done. But I want you catching them for the right reasons."

"I consider it a privilege to help protect people, Sheriff."

The sheriff coughed and pointed to the glass of water on the washstand beside the bed. Cord picked up the glass and handed it to the sheriff as his wife poked her head in the doorway.

"Do you need anything, Percy?" she asked.

The sheriff lifted his palm out toward her. "I'll be all right," he said, and she disappeared around the corner. "I understand you want to help people, but it's not your only reason. You're running, son."

"Look, if Hayden hadn't come around snooping, we wouldn't be having this conversation."

"Like I said before, I've been meaning to talk to you for some time, and now I know a few more particulars. You're good at what you do, I'll give you that, but you take too many chances."

"What I do and how I do it is my business, isn't it? We don't have a formal arrangement."

"The Lord asks us to wield the stick of the law and protect the vulnerable, but He doesn't require a human sacrifice on your part. Jesus already did the sacrificing. You need to be wise about how you catch these guys. I heard about the way you went in guns a blazing on Leroy and Carl. It's like you don't care whether you live or die, and that ain't right."

"Who told?"

"Leroy himself told me. Said he couldn't believe someone would approach them with so little cover. The surprise of it is probably what did them in."

"So what are you complaining about then, Sheriff, if what I do works?"

Belle bustled into the room. "Percy, it's time to take your medicine." She pulled the cork on a bottle of Dill's Cough Syrup and poured a liquid the color of molasses onto a spoon.

The sheriff slurped the liquid off the spoon and swallowed. "Foul tasting stuff," he sputtered, "and what's the point? I probably won't last until next week."

"The doc is only trying to make sure you do. One more now." The sheriff took another spoonful, and his wife put the back of her hand on his brow. "You're getting warm; I think Mr. Sweet should leave."

"I think so, too." Cord said grabbing his hat and rising from his chair.

"Sit down. We're not finished."

Cord perched himself on the edge of the chair.

"Call me if you need anything," Belle said, and left the room once more.

The sheriff's look pinned Cord like a butterfly specimen. "You think you're pleasing the Lord putting yourself at so much risk?"

"S'pose I never really thought about it." And he hadn't. These days Jesus seemed a long way off. When he'd mentioned the Lord to Alda the day before, he'd surprised himself.

"That's what I'm worried about. You act like you've got nothing to lose."

Alda's pretty face with a sprinkle of freckles across her upturned nose and a mountain of fiery hair crossed his mind. "Maybe I don't."

"You said you knew Jesus. That means you got a life worth living. Give yourself time to tell others about Him."

Cord fidgeted with the edge of his cowboy hat.

"And now I know you got a family who cares about you."

"Look, coming around and interfering in my business does not mean they care. My father said I was never to darken his door again."

"So maybe he's had a change of heart. You're not above forgiving, are you? A man needs his family."

"I'm getting along fine."

"That's my point; you're not. You stopped caring, and now it's like you've got a death wish. I hate to see it."

The sheriff was right. Since Cord had been chasing bounties, he'd taken unnecessary risks many a time. It was a wonder he was still breathing. "So what are you suggesting? I go home, make things right with my father, and re-enlist? After that, marry my mother's choice of a bride, and spend the rest of my days absolutely miserable?" Cord clenched his jaw to still the pulse of blood rushing through his veins. The thought of it made him want to bolt from the room, jump on his horse, and ride until he ran out of prairie.

"Forgive him, Cord; that's what I'm saying."

"Forgive him?" Cord huffed. "To hear the family talk, I'm the one who needs forgiving."

"What's Jesus telling you?"

That was a question he'd have to spend some time on. It was hard to remember the last time he'd prayed.

"I'll let you think on that, son. I'm tired." The sheriff's eyelids drooped and closed. "There's an envelope for you in the top drawer of the bureau, the bounty on Felix. Take it before you go."

"Sheriff, I don't — "

"Take it." The words were muttered and then the sheriff started up a clamor of snoring.

Cord rose, crossed to the highboy against the wall at the end of the bed, and opened the top drawer. The sheriff's shiny service revolver lay in its holster across a collection of socks, braces, and hankies. He picked up the white envelope in the corner with his name printed in a neat hand and stuffed it in his vest pocket. Somehow he'd have to convince Alda to take her share. Cord slipped from the room and bid a polite farewell to Mrs. Richards before leaving and making his way back to the sheriff's office.

Lord, I know me and You haven't talked for some time now. I need some advice on the situation with my father. Do You want me to go back home and reconcile, live the life they chose for me?

He stepped through the door of the office and found the deputies in the same state as he'd left them. The aroma of Felix lingered in the room. "Any chance I could get an escort for a young woman headed to California?"

The thin deputy spoke up, "An escort? What'd she do?"

"She didn't do anything. She needs protection."

"So someone's after her?" another deputy asked.

"No, she's driving a pack string of mules to Death Valley."

The men looked at him like he'd grown horns out the side of his head.

"Never mind," Cord said. He left the building and thumped down the front walk. *Just so you know, Lord, I won't be going home until I figure out what to do with a certain female mule skinner.*

Chapter Five

Alda lay back in the cool water of the pool under the falls. Extending her arms in a wide arc, she stared up at the cotton boll clouds in the sky. Cord had left camp in a hurry, like he was angry. Felix complained the whole way past the willows about Cord not taking the cuffs off.

What kind of a cowboy carries cuffs anyway? There'd been no sign of a badge on Cord's vest.

After fifteen minutes of scrubbing her skin nearly raw, Felix's scent no longer lingered. The man needed help. He wouldn't even look at her when she asked him why he'd attacked her. Cord handled Felix extra rough after that, and he'd put up a big fuss about being maltreated. What did Felix think she felt like — him coming after her like that?

Alda rose from the pool, water from her thick hair fanned down her back. She twisted the heavy curls to ring them out and grabbed her towel from the smooth rocks. A gentle breeze tickled her skin as she dried off.

The loaded mules raised their heads from munching the thick grasses and turned their big, soulful eyes her direction.

"I know, it'll be hard to leave this place. We won't be finding feed so rich for some time."

Charlie curled his lips back over his teeth to express his disapproval.

"You know what I'm saying, don't you, boy? Sometimes it seems like you know what I'm thinking, too."

As the morning sun crossed the sky, from Bessie's saddle, Alda viewed the rolling hills of scrub prairie dotted with gatherings of willows. The mule appeared to have fully recuperated from her colic the day before.

After crossing the river upstream from Alcove Springs, the road proved sound enough, and they made good time. According to her map, the trail would follow the Little Blue for several days. The provisions would last for eight weeks if she was careful. It would be enough time to reach Death Valley if she pushed the string.

Alda rolled her shoulders to ease the knots pulling across her back and glanced down the line before giving Bessie a reassuring pat on the neck. "You're doing good, Bessie."

Staring across knoll upon knoll along the road sent Alda into reflection. She lifted the locket from her chest and held it to her lips. *Mamma, I miss you. I'm so sorry I didn't do more when your health failed. I should have gone to the doctor long before I did. If I could take back the last few months, I would. What was I thinking, letting Pa cart me around the countryside to show off the "superior dexterity and hauling ability" of our mules when you were at home suffering. I should've been there taking care of you. I shouldn't have minded when you said, "Go on now; I'll be fine."*

A tear slid down Alda's cheek, and she scrubbed at it with her fist. She'd been played the fool by her pa too long. It was a wonder she'd never seen it before, how selfish the man was. Whenever they met someone new, he would puff out his chest and strut around on his bandy legs like some sort of rooster. And then he'd brag about having the best mules in the entire country. What good was it if you never intended to let them prove themselves?

"That's all going to change now, Bessie. When you get to hauling borax, you're going to show them all how it's done."

Bessie nodded her head as though in agreement.

The late afternoon carried a cool breeze, and Alda swatted at the occasional mosquito landing on her arm. Dark clouds rolled in the distance, and sporadic lightning flashed over thickets clustered along the shallow streams.

"Looks like we might be in for a change of weather." Alda shifted her hips in the saddle relieving the sharp pain extending down her left leg. Bringing her canteen to her lips, she swallowed several mouthfuls of spring water, still fresh from the morning, and wiped her upper lip with the back of her hand.

Half an hour later, brown clouds of mosquitoes dove for any bare skin they could find. Itchy welts formed on her face and neck.

The mules grew antsy — their ears twitching back and forth — and yanked at their leads, causing the entire string to jerk and buckle. A lightning bolt flashed behind her, and a crack of thunder shook the ground like a freight train.

Henry, the fourth mule back, reared up and pawed at the air.

"Settle down, boy, it's just a little thunder. We'll be all right; you've seen worse. Come along now …" Alda kept up the low sing song to keep the mules quiet.

Bessie pinned her ears to her head.

A bolt of lightning hit the ground directly in front of the mules, and thunder boomed from the heavens. The pack string startled and twisted in on itself as the sky opened up and dropped a curtain of rain on their backs.

"Whoa, now!" Alda screamed. The wind carried her voice away. She jumped from the saddle and slapped Moses's hind end to get him back in line.

The mule kicked out a hind hoof, catching Charlie on the flank. Bessie lifted her chin and let out a bellow before hopping forward and yanking the lead attached to her saddle. The knot of mules tightened.

Alda heaved at Old Joe's lead as a bolt of lightning

flashed.

Charlie lost his footing as Moses dropped his hindquarters and slid. The rope slackened and looped around Charlie's neck and under his chin. As the thunder crashed, the string yanked and the mules pulled away from one another, tightening the noose around Charlie's neck.

Alda gripped Moses's rope and dug her heels into the sand to jerk him back. Her hands slipped on the wet rope, and a burn tore through both palms. "Moses, back!" she screamed and yanked again and again on the lead. The mule didn't shift. Where had she packed the knife?

Charlie fell over sideways, and the rope pulled tighter around his neck.

Alda screamed and kicked at Moses, jamming her shoulder into the mule's chest as the rain poured into her eyes and ran in rivulets down her neck.

The pull on Moses's lead from Bessie's saddle kept him from moving back.

Alda returned to Old Joe and tugged on his bridle. Her heel lost its footing, and she went down on one knee. Old Joe couldn't budge with the stress of the ropes pulling on him from both directions.

Charlie's neck strained against the rope — his eyes bulged in their sockets.

"Charlie!" Alda yelled and ran to kneel in the mud and lift his head into her arms. She pried her scratched and bleeding fingers under the rope around his neck and heaved.

The mules shifted, and the rope gained a bit of slack. Charlie's head lolled into Alda's lap.

"Charlie, no, no, no … Charlie!" Alda said, wrapping her arms around the mule's neck and burying her face in his wet coat. Rain gushed over her head and soaked her back.

The mule didn't move.

"I'm so sorry. I'm so sorry, Charlie." Alda said as her

tears mixed with the rain streaming down her face.

Six hours later, Alda tossed the final rock on the mound of Charlie's grave. Straightening her back, she brushed a sopping curl off her brow. Water and grit covered her from head to toe. The rain hadn't let up for the first two hours of digging. Her arms quaked in the chill of the air. Alda wrapped her arms around her soaked shoulders and looked across the rolling hills — mud, as far as she could see.

She picked up the spade and walked over toward the other eight mules standing hodge podge around Charlie's pack. She tossed the spade into the muck and tugged her tent out of Jenny's pack. The mules could fend for themselves until morning. She needed to sleep. Alda flung her tent onto a small rise and climbed in.

~

Cord noted the mules milling about what looked like a couple of packs from a quarter mile back. No sign of Alda. He nudged Boss into a gallop. As he drew closer, one pack appeared to be a crumpled up tent.

He pulled his horse up alongside the skittish, loaded mules and dismounted. The shovel sitting in the mud must have been for the fresh grave about fifteen feet away — there were only eight mules. He shouldn't have stayed in town so long. He knew the storm would be trouble.

Dark clouds rolled in the sky, and the wind whipped across the rough prairie. Alda's bonnet lay near-buried in the mud next to a mule's hoof print. He scooped it from the ground. Where could she have gone? He strode over to the tent and lifted the front peak from the mud. The canvas parted, and water flowed onto Alda's mud-streaked face. Her bottle-green eyes blinked open.

"Alda, what are you doing? What happened?"

"Go away."

"Did you lose a mule in the storm?" He shouldn't have left her.

"Go away. I don't want to talk about it." She curled up

into a tight ball.

Alda's damp shoulders shivered. "All right, we won't talk about it, but you can't stay like this. You'll catch your death of cold."

"Then I won't be any worse off than Charlie," she whispered. "Go away, please."

Cord knelt on one knee in the mud. "You know I can't do that." He reached out a hand, pulled back, and reached out again to take a muddy curl and tuck it behind her ear.

Alda closed her eyes.

She looked like a drowned kitten. Should he pick her up, wrap her in his arms, and warm her next to his chest? No, he had no right.

"I'm going to light a fire and cook up some rabbit. I shot one on the way. You'll need to warm yourself, get your strength back, all right?" He rubbed the back of his finger across her cheek, and a shock of heat tingled up his arm. "I found your bonnet." He laid it on the canvas near her head. "You need to keep better track of this thing." He couldn't resist brushing another damp curl off her forehead. "I'm going to give you my jacket to warm you while you're waiting." Cord removed his slicker and arranged it over Alda. He tucked it under her shoulder before putting the tent back over her.

Using some dry twigs and sticks he kept in his pack, he lit a small fire on a knoll.

The flames popped and crackled as Alda drug herself out of the tent and over to the fire with his coat wrapped about her narrow shoulders.

He threw his saddle blanket down next to the fire. "Sit nice and close. I'll get some coffee on and then unload the mules."

Alda collapsed on the blanket. "It was a stupid idea, wasn't it?"

"Lying in your tent soaking wet? Yes, it was."

Alda lifted one curved eyebrow. "You're vexing me,

Mr. Cord. You know what I mean."

Cord poked at the fire and placed a blue coffee pot near the fire to heat. "Am I to understand you would like to talk about the situation now?"

Alda sighed and dropped her eyes to the fire. "It was a stupid idea thinking I could drive the mules all the way to California. I never should have pushed my ma to make the plans with Uncle Larkin. Yesterday, I was attacked by that insane man and nearly killed or worse; and today I lost one of my best mules."

"What happened?"

"They were spooked by the storm. I've never been in lightning that close before. Charlie got caught up in the rope."

"This area's known for violent storms. I should've been here."

"Why? I'm the one who set out on this foolish undertaking, and now Charlie's dead!" Alda stood, his coat dropping from her shoulders—her fists shaking at her side. "Did you hear me? Charlie's dead, and it's all my fault!" She stomped off across the prairie, bits of mud flying into the air from the heels of her boots.

Cord unloaded the mules before taking out his knife and skinning the rabbit he'd shot on the outskirts of Marysville. He'd finished frying a few pieces in bacon fat before Alda returned and sat down next to the fire. "You good now?" he asked.

"Yeah, I'm good." Alda wrapped his coat around her shoulders once more. "That smells delicious."

Cord pierced several pieces of meat in the cast iron skillet and put them on a tin plate. He handed the plate to Alda. "How long did it take you to bury Charlie?"

"Six hours, more or less." Alda picked up a thigh from the plate and bit into it. Bacon grease ran down her chin.

"That's quite an undertaking." Cord motioned to her chin, and Alda swiped at it with her sleeve.

"It's the least I could do. Those mules depend on me, and I let them down. For all I know, I may lose every one of them before I reach Death Valley."

Cord had spent over an hour in prayer on the ride, talking to the Lord about his relationship with his father and what the Lord wanted him to do about it. He'd also talked about Alda. *Lord, what do you want me to do?* Cord cleared his throat. "I could help you out. Come along on this journey of yours, if you have a mind to let me." He took a piece of rabbit and bit into it waiting for her reply.

Alda chewed through two more mouthfuls before saying a word. "It's not your responsibility, making sure I'm safe."

"I know that."

"It's my pa's, wherever he is."

"Uh huh." Cord took another bite. Maybe it was the weather, maybe it was the company, but it was the best rabbit he'd tasted in a long while.

"So what do you want in return?" Alda fixed her pretty eyes on his.

"Pardon?" If it was proper, he'd walk over and tuck the curls off her forehead again. He licked the bacon grease from his lips.

"I'm not keeping your bed warm," she said.

Cord coughed to keep from choking on the piece of meat in his throat. What was the woman thinking? "I've got no ulterior motives. I want to make sure you get there, with the rest of your string intact, that's all."

"Why not?"

"What do you mean why not? But I thought —"

"I've seen the way you look at me."

Cord could feel the heat from his chest escaping up his neck. He swallowed.

Chapter Six

Alda shifted in Bessie's saddle and then brushed the grit from her face. Today's sun had warmed yesterday's mud by early morning, and the breeze had churned up dusty clouds. The sand burned her throat with every swallow. It didn't help that Cord kept galloping off across the scrub and then galloping back to check on her.

He'd shot an antelope earlier that morning, and they'd lunched on the fresh meat, but the man hadn't said much during the meal. He hadn't said much at all since she'd questioned his motives the day before.

And why wouldn't she? Like her pa always said, *nobody does anything for nothing.* Not that she wanted to pay much mind to her father's wisdom. It hadn't gotten the family anywhere in the past.

So what were the man's motives if he wasn't interested in taking advantage of her? At least that's what he'd sputtered after he'd turned red as a beet. Maybe she'd called his bluff, and he wasn't ready to admit it.

Or maybe he was one of those religious types. He'd said the good Lord brought him to her rescue. Even so, he must have more important things to do than escort her across the country. How did he make his living? She'd forgotten to ask him about the cuffs he'd used on Felix.

Alda turned to check on the mules. They were a bedraggled lot today — mourning the loss of Charlie – and their heads were hanging low. She hadn't been able to convince them to eat more than a few bites of feed before they broke camp.

Poor Charlie; she would miss the rascal. He was one of the original mules Pa had bought from a dealer down south. A smart fellow, too. He would let himself and the others out of the field occasionally to go for a stroll to the neighbor's yard and check out Mrs. Barnes's garden. Something she didn't appreciate at all.

Alda swatted at a pesky fly buzzing around her bonnet. Pa would be in some kind of fury when he found out how Charlie died. But how could Alda have known what would happen? The storm had sneaked up so fast. He'd probably point out that she shouldn't have been there in the first place — and that might be true.

If Cord changed his mind about helping her out, there was a good chance she might not make it or the mules either. But that simply wasn't an option. Somehow she needed to arrive in Death Valley in eight weeks with the other mules. Hopefully Uncle Larkin could find another mule to finish out a team for hauling.

Cord galloped toward her, creating another cloud of dust.

Alda pulled the collar of her blouse up to cover her mouth and nose and closed her eyes.

"You all right?" Cord asked.

Alda waited a few seconds before dropping her collar and opening her eyes. "I'd be much better off if you stopped arriving in such a rush."

Cord kept his eyes fixed on his saddle horn. "Another hour and we should be heading into The Narrows, those bluffs you see in the distance. They follow the Blue pretty tight so the trail is narrow."

"How narrow? The mules are out of sorts today," Alda winced. Her bland statement didn't come anywhere near describing the turmoil caused by the loss of dear Charlie.

"It's wide enough for a wagon. You'll be fine. We'll

take our time." Cord pulled the reins across Boss's neck and trotted off toward a thicket along a narrow creek.

An hour's ride found Cord leading Alda and the pack string into the Narrows, a lonely section of the trail tucked in between rugged hills with little vegetation. Protrusions of rock clung to the hillsides in slapdash clumps. The view was limited to the next turn on the winding trail. They stopped to water the animals at a calm spot in the river.

"It's a desolate place," Alda remarked, dismounting from Bessie.

Cord joined her in leading the mules alongside the river and allowing them to take a few slurps of water.

"Some say this stretch is haunted," Cord said.

The rough landscape lent itself to a sense of eeriness. Alda glanced over her shoulder.

"About twenty years ago, nine men were killed, some of them scalped."

"So it was Indians."

"The military had withdrawn, and the natives wanted their land back."

"Any women or children killed?"

"Two women were taken captive and a couple of children. They returned them six months later for ransom in Denver."

Alda lifted a hand to her brow and scanned the top of the bluffs.

"Not many left now. Most of them either died or the government moved them out to Indian Territory, although there are a couple of reservations along the Missouri. You might see some in Kearney; it's a bustling place these days. We'll camp this side of it tonight and pick up supplies tomorrow."

"I packed for eight weeks. I won't need to go into town tomorrow."

Cord smiled for the first time since yesterday — a welcome sight in the dreary landscape.

"As you can see, Miss Alda, I'm traveling considerably lighter than yourself." He swung a leg over Boss and pressed the horse's flanks to move on before saying over his shoulder, "A day in town will do you good. You can wear something pretty, and I'll take you to lunch."

"But — " Alda watched Cord's back as he rode out of earshot. She mounted Bessie and pressed her sides to get moving.

Something pretty? Alda looked down at her dusty and wrinkled riding skirt. There was a reason she and her ma had made several in trail brown, but it would never be considered *pretty*. She would have to look over the two dresses she'd grabbed in haste and see if either one of them would do. Cord was right; a lunch in town might be the thing to raise her spirits. Still, he was a quagmire of inconsistency. Was this an attempt to woo her?

Alda nudged Bessie to pick up the pace. The Narrows were too unnerving to allow Cord to get too far ahead.

After leaving The Narrows, the landscape formed grassy hills interspersed with stands of mixed trees along pleasant creeks. The weather was cooperating so they pushed on well into the evening and stopped to overnight several miles east of Kearney.

"I'll tend to the animals if you would like to get supper on," Cord said.

Alda was too tired to argue. Her arms and back had begun to ache like she was being stretched on a rack. If it were up to her, she'd just as soon skip the evening meal and climb into her tent. "I can make a stew if you like; antelope would suit it fine. There'll probably be some wild onions along the creek, too."

Cord dipped his black Stetson. "I'll leave you to it then," he said and led the animals down toward the thick grass along the water's edge.

Alda gathered sticks and built a fire before throwing cubes of antelope meat into sizzling fat in her Dutch oven.

After eating supper and cleaning up the dishes, Alda and Cord sat by the fire. Several times Alda had to force her eyelids open and attempt to concentrate on Cord's rambling. If she didn't go to her tent soon, she might fall asleep where she was perched. She took another sip of coffee and wrapped her hands around the mug to warm them.

It would be hard to leave the warmth of the fire. She'd pitched her tent on a hillock several yards away from the fire to let Cord know she had no intention of going back on her word. It would serve propriety better if they could find a companion to travel along with them. Perhaps she could ask around in Kearney tomorrow — see if anyone needed transportation west. And then Cord wouldn't need to be as anxious about her safety.

She stared over the rim of her mug and across the flickering flames at Cord, who was reclined on one elbow on his bedroll next to the fire. He was focused on peeling the bark off a narrow forked stick.

His eyes met hers and locked.

Alda shifted her position and took another sip.

"Are you too tired to talk? Your eyes have closed several times in the last couple of minutes." He pulled another thin strip of bark from the stick. "I was wondering if I might have to relieve you of that mug in order to avoid another calamity." His shadowed eyes sought hers once more.

A nervous giggle fluttered from her throat. "Is that your life's work, Mr. Cord, rescuing damsels in distress?"

His eyes widened for just a moment before his gaze dropped back to the stick. "Not in so many words, but in a way I suppose."

Alda sat up straighter. In a way? What way and exactly how many damsels were there? "Are you some kind of a lawman? I noticed you had Felix in cuffs. They're not the usual cowboy gear."

"Yes, I'm some sort of lawman." His answer was hesitant, drawn-out.

"You are? What kind of a lawman cavorts around the prairie helping women with their mules?"

"I'm a bounty hunter."

"Bounty hunter?" Coffee sloshed over the side of her mug and onto her fingers. She wiped them on the edges of her skirt. "That's dangerous, isn't it?"

"Probably no more dangerous than trying to keep you safe."

"Touché, Mr. Cord." He wouldn't distract her with his humor this time. She needed some answers. "And your family? How do they feel about you putting yourself in the line of fire outside, and yet inside, the law?"

His eyes drifted slowly to hers. "They don't know."

The answer was not a surprise. It was good to know Cord had family though. Bounty hunters were known for being tough, cold men with little prospect elsewhere. Not husband material. Alda let out a slow breath. "Why the mystery? You've had plenty of opportunity to mention your line of work before now."

"I'm hoping you can keep a secret for my sake as much as yours. Not everyone approves of my line of work, and the criminal element certainly does not approve. It would put you in grave danger if word got out."

"So I'm a bit of a side job while you're chasing the bad guys?"

Cord sat up as a deep chuckle emanated from his chest. "No, Miss Alda, you're much too time consuming to be considered a side job." He rose, stretched his long legs, and sauntered over to retrieve Alda's hatchet from beside her packs. With the broad end of the hatchet, he pounded three forked sticks, about two and a half feet high, on either side of the fire.

Alda watched as he added cross pieces to each pair from the collection he'd peeled beside the fire. "Are you jerking the rest of the antelope?"

"The meat won't last if I don't. If I slice it thin, it should be done by morning."

"You'll have to stay awake to mind the fire, won't you?" There was no way Alda could do it. Once she hit the pillow, or the skirt doubling as her pillow, she'd be lucky to wake come morning.

"I haven't been sleeping much anyway." His dark eyes sought hers again.

Alda's chest warmed. The man brought up feelings in her she wasn't accustomed to.

"Would you mind if I gave you something?" he asked.

"Something you found or ..."

"Something I picked up in Marysville the other day."

Why would Cord be shopping for her in Marysville? "You bought me a gift?"

"A useful sort of gift, I suppose."

"You have my interest piqued, Mr. Cord."

"So is that a yes?"

"Yes, you may give me your gift." The man was hard to figure out. One minute it felt like he was attracted to her, and the next minute it didn't.

Cord left the fire and walked to where he'd piled his supplies. He returned with a leather scabbard and laid it across her knees.

Alda ran her hands down the length of the smooth leather and straightened the fringe. With one finger, she traced the three beautifully tooled letters between the patterns on either end. *Red.* The same nickname her pa called her, the pa who'd taken off and left her when mamma died. Cord couldn't have known though.

"It's for your shot gun," he said. "I thought it would come in handy when you needed to shoot someone."

"Thank you. It's beautiful, but I'm hoping I can leave the shooting up to you."

Cord's eyes took on a haunted look at her remark. "I'll

check on the livestock while you make your way to your tent. Good night," he said, and turned his back to walk away.

Alda's gaze flitted toward the white triangle reflecting the moon's glow in the clear night. "Good night …Cord."

He stopped and looked over his shoulder. The glow of the fire lit up one side of his face — softening his features as he grinned. "I'll see you in the morning," he said and nodded.

Chapter Seven

The sidewalks of Wyoming Avenue pulsed as citizens accomplished their morning business in Kearney. Women carried stacks of brown paper parcels and scurried from store to store. A thin, young boy wearing short pants and a tweed cap stood on the corner shouting out the headlines from the day's newspaper.

Cord stopped and handed the boy a nickel in exchange for a paper, rolled it quickly, and placed it under his arm. Continuing down the sidewalk, he gripped Alda's elbow. She glanced back with a raised eyebrow. Taking several long strides, he caught the edge of her dress, and she almost stumbled. "Sorry."

"Are we in a hurry, Mr. Cord?"

Back to the formal address, the thaw from the night before was apparently over. "I'll slow down. The chophouse is only another half block."

Cord heard the newsie yell out that the Doc Rufus gang struck again. Two more people were killed in a bungled train robbery ten miles further west. The news made him churlish. The town was too busy for his liking.

Built around the connections of several rail lines, it smelled of oil and burnt coal, which always made his eyes water. Why had he even mentioned having lunch with Alda? They could've made good time if they'd skirted the town as she'd suggested.

Of course, seeing her emerge from the tent that morning

had made it all worth it. She'd cut a striking figure standing in the sun's rays—wearing a dress the same green as her eyes. A pity she'd covered her gorgeous curls with another bonnet.

Get a hold of yourself, man. Alda was right; he'd been looking at her like he wanted to drink her in, and it wasn't right. *Lord, help me*. She deserved his respect. The closeness of their travels was making it difficult to maintain his distance. He'd never met a woman so plucky and beautiful at the same time. His line of work didn't allow for relationships; he would have to make that clear over lunch.

Cord stopped at The Beckett House. They entered the hotel, and he directed Alda to the dining room. Turning the brass knob, he said, "After you, Miss."

Alda tucked her chin down; a smile played at the corners of her mouth as she stepped through the door. "Why thank you, Sir."

A young woman seated them at a table for two by the window. The place was fancier than he was used to. Billowy curtains lined the windows, and glass domes displayed a bunch of impressive desserts on the counter — most likely more money for less food.

"I'm suitably impressed. I didn't know you were a patron of such establishments."

He glanced over at Alda. Was she giving him a compliment? She nibbled at the corner of her lip and then continued to study her menu. The company made the change of his usual venue worth it. Perhaps he would have the roasted wild goose.

Alda put her menu on the table. "Are you trying to hide something?"

"Hide something?" Cord glanced out the window. What did she expect him to say?

"In the newspaper." She pointed to the paper rolled up and pressed against the table with his elbow.

"Uhhmm. Not particularly." The way his voice rose was a sure giveaway, but the less she knew the better.

"I can handle the news, Mr. Cord. Is it about the gang who robbed the train?"

"It's a sad story, that one," the waitress interrupted, pencil poised to take their order. "Word is these scoundrels have no problem killing men, women, or children. In the last robbery, they shot a small boy because he wouldn't stop crying."

Alda's face turned as white as the tablecloth.

"I don't mean to scare you, Ma'am, but it makes folks around here nervous."

"If you could take our order, please, and maybe a cold glass of water for the lady to start."

Alda needed something quick. She looked like she might keel over on the table.

"My advice — "

"If you could take our order." Cord smiled his best. It had been known to stop some women in their tracks.

The waitress's smile slipped from her face. "My advice, if you're traveling, make sure it's not alone. You never know what these scoundrels might be up to next."

The woman was apparently oblivious to his charms. Cord flashed the waitress a warning look and then smiled at Alda. "What would you like to order?"

Alda's fingers shook as she picked up the menu. "I think I'll have the pressed corned beef cold dish, thank you."

"And you, Sir?"

The woman did a fine impression of the evil eye. "I'll have the wild goose. Is that à la Fermière or in traditional style?" Cord raised one eyebrow so she would know he expected an answer.

"Uuuh, traditional, I believe." The waitress snatched the menu from his hand and reached out for Alda's. "I'll bring you a nice cup of Earl Grey to start, Ma'am."

"If you would be so kind."

"And I will take that cold glass of water."

As the waitress left to fill their order, one tear escaped down Alda's cheek, and she wiped it with her gloved hand.

He leaned back in his chair and put the newspaper on his lap.

"I guess I can't handle the news very well. What would possess a grown man to hurt a child?"

"I'm sure I don't know. I wish it didn't happen, ever."

"The poor mother, how devastated she must be. The horror of seeing your child murdered before your eyes. Tell me, Mr. Cord, why are these things allowed to happen?"

"Why does God allow them? Is that your question?"

"Yes, why would a loving God allow an innocent child to die in such atrocious circumstances?"

"Uuhhmm." Where was the waitress with his water? "I would say it wasn't the Lord's will the child should die."

Alda bent forward with a furrowed brow. "Then why did it happen?" she asked. "Why do terrible things happen while others are left to suffer the consequences?"

A difficult question. He opened his mouth to speak.

"It's not fair." Alda dropped her fist to the table, shaking the vase of flowers and rattling the silverware.

Several patrons at the other tables turned toward her outburst. Cord raised his palms out and managed a smile, and they turned back to their luncheon.

Alda seemed overly upset. Maybe her distress wasn't all about the little boy. "Are you talking about your mother or the little boy?"

Alda leaned back, and her shoulders crumpled. "Either, I suppose. Would you kindly answer my question?"

"Alda, are you not a believer?"

"I'm not sure." Her voice was barely a whisper.

"But you prayed with me — at our meals together."

"I listened to you pray. It's your business if you believe."

Give yourself time to tell others about Him. The sheriff's words crossed his mind. *Lord, give me wisdom.* "Alda," he said quietly, "look at me."

She lifted her head; the vivid green of her eyes were clouded with moisture.

"I believe in a God Who loves me and Who loves you. Life can be difficult and painful, but what we see is not all there is. Someday, Jesus will take us to live with Him for all eternity." Cord reached across the table and wrapped his hand around hers. "The Bible says 'He will wipe every tear from our eye, and there will be no more sorrow and no more pain.' God never intended for sickness or for cruelty to be a part of our lives. We chose it, when we went our own way."

Alda dropped her chin to her chest.

"God doesn't ask much from us either — He just wants you to … love Him back." *Lord, please help her see.* He gave her hand a squeeze. "He's not like your father. Jesus will never leave you or forsake you."

"I don't wish to talk about my pa."

Cord released her hand as the waitress arrived with their meal, and they made small talk as they ate their lunch.

Alda met his eyes during their servings of bread pudding smothered in caramel sauce. "I think it would be best if we joined with others traveling west. I wouldn't be as much of a responsibility to you, and you would be more at liberty to do your work."

It was a good idea. It would solve the problem of their becoming too close, but he would miss having her to himself. "I'll stop in at the General Store and ask around. More than likely, there will be some sort of caravan heading out of town. The next three hundred fifty miles to Laramie are difficult. There's not a lot of water, and the land is pretty barren." Why was Alda frowning — almost like she was disappointed? It was her idea. "I still want to help you."

Alda's eyes brightened.

"With your mules, it's a lot of responsibility."

She slowly closed her eyes and opened them. "I look forward to your assistance."

An hour later, at the General Store, Cord learned of a six wagon train, led by a father and son, continuing on to Oregon the next morning. He tracked down the father who agreed to let them join their party for fifty dollars. He paid the man and made arrangements to meet and depart from the stockyards on the west end of town.

Two hours after sunrise the next morning, Cord slowed Boss's gait to keep pace with Alda and the string on the road. She commented on the cows and sheep staked along the way. He told her it was to keep them from roaming yet allow them to feed on the sparse grass. The country didn't hold much for trees either. The mules hadn't cooperated with being loaded at sunrise as they'd been spooked by the trains passing every few minutes. They'd been delayed by over an hour. A hand at the stockyards informed Cord the group had moved on before Cord and Alda had arrived and would look for them to catch up.

Dark circles ringed Alda's eyes, and her face was more pale than usual. "If you don't mind me saying, you look a little worse for wear this morning."

The corners of Alda's mouth turned up in a wry smile. "Why thank you for the compliment, Mr. Cord. You do know how to bring cheer to a woman's heart."

So maybe he didn't need to say it, but she didn't need to be so sensitive. He was concerned about her, that's all. "You didn't sleep well?"

Alda's cheeks puffed, and she blew out a breath of air. "No, I did not sleep well. You gave me a lot to think about at yesterday's lunch, and that's what I did — think about it."

It was good to know she was mulling his words over, but he wasn't going to pry. She'd come round to asking him questions when she was good and ready. "A fine day for travel."

Alda tilted her head his direction and raised an eyebrow. "Yes, a fine day for travel."

"It will slow our progress — traveling with the wagons."

"Are you having regrets about making the arrangements?"

Cord scratched at a bite on his cheek. "Nope. It will be safer for you."

"When you have to leave, you mean, and do your bounty hunting work."

"Yes, about that, you can't mention it to anyone. My success depends upon my
anonymity." Not only his success, but it also kept him from being hunted down and killed.

"I won't tell. Do you mind telling me how successful you've been?"

"I've been supporting myself for two years. It's a good living… a very good living." A good living if you don't mind putting yourself in danger and not having a place to lay your head.

"What did you do before bounty hunting?"

"Why all the questions?"

Alda's eyes sparkled as she grinned. "I'm trying to make conversation. We won't have as much opportunity to do so when we travel with the others."

That would be a good thing. He didn't like to talk about himself. Most people didn't notice, as they were happy enough talking about themselves. Alda was different, though, she seemed to have a genuine interest in him, but how much he should tell her? "I was a soldier."

"A soldier?"

"You could say it's in the blood. My family has served for four generations. In fact, my father's still in the military."

"Are you a deserter, Mr. Cord?"

It was difficult to keep the sarcasm from his voice. "No, I'm not a deserter. I received an honorable discharge at my own request. But as far as my family's concerned, I abandoned my true calling and brought shame to them in the process." Just saying the words made his stomach twist. He'd been praying about forgiving his father ever since the sheriff suggested it. Apparently it hadn't taken hold yet.

"So you're hiding out?"

"No, I'm not hiding out." Cord prodded Boss into a canter and pulled away from the string — he needed a break from all the talk.

Six covered wagons, the curve of their canvas tops bright white against the sandy soil of the Platte River Basin, spread along the trail a couple of miles outside of Kearney. About three hundred cattle followed the wagons and were driven by Silas Parsons, the man Cord met the day before, and two others.

Silas turned his horse from the cattle and rode back to meet Cord and Alda. The fellow was shy of five and a half feet and several rolls poked out from under his leather vest. His face split into a grin below a handlebar mustache spanning as far as any Cord had ever seen. "Hello, folks, I'm glad to see you caught up with us. The others were anxious to head out bright and early this morning. We had a couple of days rest in Kearney, and I imagine by about day three the enthusiasm will be wearing off again." Silas's shoulders shook as he chuckled at his own comment.

Cord tipped his hat. "We appreciate you letting us tag along. Silas Parsons, Miss Alda Lealand."

Silas appraised Alda as he twisted the waxed tip of his mustache. "Nice to meet you, Miss," he said, and tipped his dusty brown Stetson. Several chunks of the brim were missing like a horse had considered his hat a breakfast.

"So nice to meet you, too, Mr. Parsons. We will feel much safer traveling in a larger group."

She was speaking for herself. The only thing he would feel safer about was spending too much time alone with her.

"It will be a pleasure to have someone as experienced as yourselves along the trail. The others are green. One of the fellows is a pastor; another one is a journalist. I'm not sure how long they're going to hold out."

"It wouldn't be the truth, Mr. Parsons, if you thought me experienced." Alda glanced away and fidgeted with Bessie's reins. "I've been on the trail for less than a week."

"Oh, my mistake, I thought …" Silas looked to Cord.

It wasn't any of Silas's business what Cord's and Alda's travel arrangements were. He wasn't so sure what they were himself.

Alda glanced over as though she expected him to comment.

"We'll stay in the rear until you stop for your noon meal," Cord said.

"All right, you can meet the others then." Silas turned his horse and galloped back to the herd.

Alda clucked to Bessie, and the mule moved down the road.

"Hold up for a bit. We don't want to be eating dust all morning."

"In that case I think I'll walk for a bit." Alda slid from Bessie's back. "My muscles could use some stretching." She walked in the sand holding Bessie by the reins. "What did you tell Mr. Parsons our circumstances were? He seemed to think I was experienced on the trail."

"I didn't tell him much. I didn't know much. You never actually said you wanted me to look out for you." Most likely the woman was too proud. But now he had a good reason to stay close-by. He wanted to make sure Alda's questions about the Lord were answered.

"You're right. I never did say."

Chapter Eight

Cord was correct; following the wagons was considerably slower than traveling with the two of them. The mules snorted their disdain at the lack of green grass and sneaked any mouthfuls of thistle they could get away with. Alda wiped the dust from her cheeks and forehead with the back of her sleeve and brushed the front of her riding skirt. A small cloud of dust bloomed from the dark folds.

Bits of yesterday's lunch conversation played over and over in her mind as she walked the trail alongside the mules. Cord said God loved her—the same thing mamma had told her since she was a little girl. Believing it was hard, especially when your pa didn't agree. Mamma had told her more than once she should've never married someone so set against the Lord. The unequal yoke was almost too much to bear. Maybe that's why she hadn't fought — at the end. Maybe she'd given up hope that Alda and her Pa would ever *love God back,* like Cord said. If Cord believed like he said he did, she couldn't even consider burdening him with her unbelief. He deserved someone who felt the same way about the Lord.

Shortly before sundown, Alda led the mules up to the edge of the snug circle formed by the wagons around a central campfire. Several women flitted back and forth between the wagons and the fire to prepare the evening meal.

"Howdy, Ma'am."

Alda looked up at the speaker. A tall, wide shouldered man sat atop a saddle on a sleek black Arabian with a snip of white down its nose. He was one of the three she'd watched herding cattle all day. The horse was even more magnificent in close quarters.

Alda reached out and patted the neck of the horse. It turned its head and nuzzled at her fingers with its wet nose, looking for a treat as she spoke. "What a beautiful horse. What's his name?"

The fellow laughed and reached forward to shake her hand. "The name's Prince. The horse's name I mean, and if you care to know mine, it's Walker. This might be a first, giving the horse's name before my own. My father and I are heading up the wagon train to Oregon. It's a pleasure to meet you."

Alda put her hand in Walker's. He didn't look much like his dad. Curly blond hair peeked out from under his hat. High cheekbones, bronzed by the sun, complemented his aquiline nose and dimpled chin.

His china blue eyes sparkled. "Ma'am?"

Alda dropped his fingers. "Sorry." A warm flush gathered at her chest. She raised her hand to cover the color inching its way up her neck.

"If you're wondering, I take after my mother. Her family was Swedish." Walker's bright smile spread across his face. "You must be Mrs. Cord."

"P-pardon?"

"Cord's wife; he didn't give his last name."

Why would he think she was Cord's wife? "I'm not Cord's wife."

"You're not?" Walker cleared his throat and shifted in his saddle.

It was hopeless now. She could feel the blush wash over her face and disappear into her hair. Most likely they were about the same color right now. "I can assure you, it's not what you are thinking. Mr. Cord is merely assisting me on my journey."

"I see, *your* journey."

"Yes, *my* journey."

"*Your* journey to where?"

"I'm headed to Death Valley. I have an uncle waiting for me to show up with the mules. He made a deal with the Eagle Borax Company to buy them and use them for hauling."

Walker removed his hat and scratched his head. Several curls fell across his forehead, and he tucked them behind his ear. "So you were headed to California, on your own, with a pack string?"

Alda exhaled a breath. Gorgeous or not, the man asked a lot of questions. "Yes, perhaps not the best idea." Her thoughts ran to Charlie. "But I embarked on the journey alone. Mr. Cord has been kind enough to provide help several times along the way." The words sounded inadequate as soon as she uttered them.

"I'll bet he has," Walker drawled and returned his hat to his head. "If you like, I can help you unload the mules, and they can graze with the cattle."

Alda searched the circle for Cord. He appeared engrossed in a conversation with a slim fellow wearing a ridiculous black top hat on the other side of the fire. She gave Walker a quick smile. "Thank you. It would be most appreciated."

"Tchick, tchick, come on Bessie; let's get these packs off," Alda said, and pivoted Bessie's neck so the string could follow Walker out onto the dusky prairie.

Footfalls landed behind her on the sand. "Alda, wait up." Cord said. "I can help you unload the mules."

Alda faced Cord. The questioning eyebrows, the curve of his strong jaw, his kindness—she missed him already. "Walker's going to help me, but I appreciate your offer."

"Walker?"

"Silas's son. You haven't met him yet?"

"He hasn't had the opportunity until now," Walker said and prompted his horse forward out of the shadows.

Cord looked up at Walker and then over to her and then back to Walker.

She hadn't done anything wrong, yet the pit of her stomach burned.

"Nice to meet you, Mr., uhhh, Cord," Walker said as he raised his hat and nodded his head. "I am glad you've decided to travel with us. Pa said you'd be a hand with the cattle if one of us is otherwise," Walker looked over at Alda, "engaged."

Cord glared back with tightness around the eyes she hadn't seen before. "I imagine I can be of some use. I'll leave you two to the unloading," he said, and stalked back across the sand toward the wagons.

"What's his problem? You said he was merely assisting you."

"I'm bone tired, Walker. Could we unload the mules so I can set up my tent?"

"I can help you with that, too."

"You don't need to bother. You've helped enough already." Alda stepped forward and tugged on Bessie's lead. "Come on, girl. The sooner you're unloaded, the sooner I can go to sleep."

Bessie nudged the back of Alda's shoulder as she led them toward the cattle dotting the scabby landscape.

Later that evening, Alda stared into the fire as the flames twisted and twirled under the Dutch oven over the fire. Removing her sock, she rubbed the angry blisters along her toes. Walking all day hadn't been such a good idea.

A tall slip of a woman with coal black hair pulled into a loose bun stepped over to the pot hanging over the fire and lifted the lid. "It looks like the men have almost picked the pot clean," she said with a pretty Irish lilt in her voice.

"You don't want to be late coming to supper with this troop. I can scrape the sides of the pot if you like. It looks like you have some nasty blisters."

Alda looked at yesterday's biscuits sitting beside her on a tin plate. They'd be crumbly and even tougher than yesterday. She'd been too tired to make anything else, and Cord had said he'd look out for himself. "If you can manage to find some, it would be much appreciated. It took longer than usual to unload the mules." That and Walker had taken his sweet time helping. She could have unloaded them faster by herself.

The ladle scraped on the bottom of the pot as the woman scooped a small serving onto a tin plate and then handed it to Alda. "Eat up. You need to put some meat on those bones," she said as she flopped down on the horse blanket next to Alda and adjusted her skirt to cover her boots.

"Thank you, this smells wonderful. As to putting meat on my bones, it would appear you don't take your own advice." Alda took a large spoonful of the turnips and potatoes.

Melodic laughter sprung from the woman's lips. "I've heard those words my whole life along with *We need to fatten you up. You're slim as a whistle.* But I've never had the opportunity to return them, until now. My name's Bridget MacDarby; nice to meet you."

Alda put her spoon down and reached out to shake Bridget's hand. "Alda Lealand; it's nice to meet you, too. Traveling with you folks will be a pleasure if it includes meals like this one. I'm assuming you made the stew. It's delicious."

"The women like to take turns — give each other a rest. Two or three of us usually pull the evening meal together. There won't be any more of my world-famous stew, though. We butchered the last of the sheep a couple of days ago. It's a relief not having to mind them."

Two young girls ran up to Bridget, one with waist length wavy, blond hair, and the other with straight, black hair. "Mamma, Pa said we had to go to bed now, but I told him we had to wait for you." The blond one spoke in a rush.

"Girls, your manners. This is Miss Lealand."

The girls smiled and curtsied. "A pleasure to meet you," they said in unison.

"Miss Lealand, these are my twins." Bridget motioned toward the dark-haired girl first. "Ruby and Pearl."

Alda smiled, "What lovely names for lovely, little girls."

Pearl clasped her tiny hands and grinned while Ruby slipped behind her sister and peered over her shoulder.

"You girls, go on now. If your pa said to get ready for bed then get ready for bed. I'll be over shortly to tuck you in."

The girls scampered off in the direction of one of the wagons.

"What sweet little girls," Alda said.

"They turned five two weeks ago and keep us hopping most days. Sometimes I don't think my husband Grey knew what hit him, from a confirmed bachelor to three females trying to run his life."

"Where are you from?"

"If you haven't guessed, I'm originally from Ireland. I moved to Springfield about seven years ago after I was hired as a school teacher. You can see how that turned out." Bridget pressed a hand to her mouth to stifle her giggles.

Alda couldn't help but giggle along with her.

"Grey wants more land, and he wants it cheap. We sold our sheep farm and most of our belongings earlier this spring. We have family in Oregon and thought it would be an adventure, let alone much cheaper, to join the Parsons' train and go west."

"Cheaper for sure; I'm not so sure about the adventure

part."

"I know what you're saying. There are many days I wonder why I got myself into this."

Cord approached them carrying his coffee pot and two mugs. "Ladies, I made a fresh pot and thought you might like some before it's gone."

Alda hadn't seen him since he'd stalked off earlier in the evening. Was he bringing her a peace offering? She shouldn't encourage his attention. It wouldn't be fair. The rich smell of the coffee reached her nostrils. "I don't — "

"Mr. Cord, you make a woman's dreams come true."

Cord smiled, and the corners of his eyes softened. "I don't know about that, but I'd be happy to share my pot with you. You'll have to ask Miss Lealand here, but I think I've got the brewing down to an art."

Cord glanced over as though seeking her approval. It was true. His coffee was delicious. Alda smiled at Cord, and a look of relief passed over his features. "You spoil me, Mr. Cord." He handed her a cup and poured the steamy black liquid. "I'll have to learn your secret before our travels end."

The coffee stream wobbled slightly, and Alda looked up into Cord's eyes. He had resumed the steel mask from earlier in the evening. He would have to get used to her pushing him away. Even if she'd much rather take his hand in hers and share secrets by the fire.

Alda dropped her lips to the rim of the cup and took a long sip. She closed her eyes as the smooth coffee slid down her throat.

He poured Bridget a cup.

"What a blessed treat. Thank you. The girls will have to do without me. I am going to enjoy this coffee."

"You're welcome," Cord said as his footsteps retreated across the sand.

Alda took another sip.

"If I wasn't married, I would snatch that man up in a

minute."

Alda's eyes blinked open.

Bridget took a drink from her mug. "Mmmm, mmm. Anyone who looks that fine and can brew a pot of coffee like this … is a keeper." She jabbed Alda in the ribs. Alda leaned to the side to keep her coffee from spilling on her skirt.

"I think there's a whole lot more to a relationship than good looks and a good cup of coffee." Like maybe the same feelings about God.

"He's a good man. Loves the Lord."

Precisely.

"He spent the afternoon talking to Grey. And the Lord knows Grey needed to talk to another man. Day after day on the wagon — following the rear end of the one in front of you, and your young'uns asking a million questions. It can wear on a man. We were happy to have him alongside. Cord told us about your plans."

"Did they sound as foolish to you as they do to everyone else?"

Bridget tipped her head and pinched her chin. "Foolish? I'm not so sure about that. Brave? Definitely."

Brave sounded a lot better than stubborn. She'd have to remember that when talking to her pa. "How much did he tell you?"

"Only about your plans to travel to Death Valley and sell the pack string for your family."

"Family? Did he mention my mamma died a few days before I left and my pa lit out to some fancy sanatorium for a *well needed rest*, in his words?"

Bridget rested her hand on Alda's forearm. "No, he didn't. I'm so sorry. A person's in a sad state when they can't count on the ones they love."

Ada stared at her cup as she swirled the coffee in her mug. *A sad state*. It was a good way to describe how she felt most days.

The fire popped and snapped, shooting sparks into the blackness.

"He cares for you," Bridget said. "You can hear it in his voice when he talks about you."

Alda gouged her heel into the sand and twisted it from side to side.

"I'm not sure why that would upset you. A person can tell by the expression in your eyes that you have feelings for him, too."

Alda wouldn't deny them, but she wasn't going to do anything about them either.

"The prairie can make strange partners. Look at Virginia over there." Bridget pointed to the third wagon over.

The lantern inside the canvas created a shadow scene of a young woman with long hair down her back rocking a bundle. The woman brought the bundle near her face as though kissing it, returned it to her lap, and tucked the blankets around it.

"She's Archie and Sarah Pickett's oldest daughter. About one week into the trip, Everett Woolsey lost his wife in childbirth. The baby was a few weeks early. Why anyone would leave home that close to delivering is a mystery to me."

"So she's taking care of the child for him?" Alda couldn't do it. She'd much rather drive her stubborn mules than take care of someone else's baby.

"She married him. She's only fifteen."

"Married him?"

"Like I said earlier, Cord's a keeper. You might want to come to some sort of agreement before the decision's taken out of your hands. Good men don't last long when we're traveling so close and we have several eligible women along."

Walker appeared in the light of the fire where Bridget and Alda were sitting. He held out a palm as he spoke,

"Miss Alda, could I escort you safely to your tent."

"Now, Mr. Walker, you know Miss Alda is perfectly capable of getting to her tent all by herself."

"I'm sorry, Mrs. MacDarby, if you believed I was talking to you." Walker pinned his eyes on Bridget's as though daring her to respond.

Bridget straightened her back before she rose from the blanket and stood. She glared down at him.

"Maybe — "

"Mr. Walker," Bridget said. "I'd be happy to escort my dear friend to her tent for you. Come along, Alda."

Bridget reached down and gripped Alda's hand to lift her from the blanket. The woman was strong for such a slip of a thing.

"Good night, Mr. Walker," Alda said over her shoulder as Bridget pulled her away from the fire.

Walker glared after them, his blue eyes snapping.

Chapter Nine

Cord's eyes gravitated to Courthouse Rock in the distance, emerging from the plains like some sort of ancient edifice. Its counterpart, Jailhouse Rock, although not as tall, looked just as impressive. The two were the start of the anomalies one discovered as you headed west. Made of yellowed clay and sandstone, the towers never ceased to bring him to thoughts of the Lord and the wonders of creation. It would have been nice to talk about the Lord with Alda and see if she had done any more thinking about what he'd shared in Kearney, but she never had a minute alone. If she wasn't with Bridget or the girls, Walker was at her side until his pa shooed him back to the cattle.

Over the last week, he wanted to take the boy aside more than once and ask him to give Alda some room to collect her thoughts. But it was like she could read his mind. If he tried pulling Walker to the side, she'd intervene and ask him to do some inane task she could do herself.

She deserved better than Walker. Never mind the boy looked like a Greek God, he couldn't fault his horse skills either, but he wasn't mature enough. Alda needed someone with strength, wisdom, someone she could depend on and who wouldn't let her down like her pa did. Someone like himself? Hard to admit but the thought of Alda with someone else, anyone else, got his insides to twisting and turning. *Lord, you know my line of work is not a fitting occupation for any husband with a family counting on him, but I'm growing fond of Alda. I need your help.*

Bridget and Grey's twins giggled from their seat in the saddle on Bessie's back. Alda had offered to take the girls at their quick lunch break and give their parents a needed rest. She looked good with the girls. Who was he kidding? He thought she looked good lying like a drowned rat in her tent.

For the most part, the folks in the train liked to lend each other a hand. So far there hadn't been much for argument other than Reverend Heaton claiming someone stole his Bible when they'd spent the night near Ogallala. Judging by the innocent look on Bridget's face the next morning, she might've had something to do with the worn, leather Bible being found in Heaton's flour sack the next day. The man fumed and fussed something awful when he discovered it. It was hard to take him serious, though, when every time he pounded the book for emphasis, a puff of flour escaped from between its pages.

Cord pulled away from the wagons and toward Alda and the mule train. The twins grew quiet as he pulled up alongside. "Mighty fine day," he said.

She smiled, and her eyes carried the same sparkle from the first day they met. "Yes, Mr. Cord, a mighty fine day."

The girls tilted their heads up and looked at him from under the curve of their bonnets. The dark one whispered in her sister's ear.

"Girls, now you know it's impolite to tell secrets. What are you whispering about?" Alda said.

"Nothing, Miss Alda."

"Come on, out with it." Alda grinned and wagged her finger at the girls. "You know your mamma would want you to be polite."

The dark haired girl shook her head from side to side.

"Pearl, what did she say?"

"She said this is the man mamma thinks you're gonna marry."

Cord wrestled with the smile threatening to split his face. "Can we assume the little one has been eavesdropping when she was supposed to be sleeping? Hard to keep a secret when you're all sleeping in the same bed."

Alda glowered at him. "I'm not sure when she heard it, but the woman needs to mind her own — "

"I'm pretty sure you don't want any disparaging words carried back." Cord nodded to the girls.

Alda glanced at the girls before biting the edge of her lip and inhaling and exhaling a deep breath. "Mr. Cord, is there a reason you came over to talk to us? I haven't seen much of you over the past week."

So she had noticed his absence. "Can't say as that was all my fault."

Alda knit her eyebrows, and a deep furrow appeared between them.

"You seemed to have a lot of company," he said.

She dropped her head and smoothed the front of her skirt with one hand. "I must admit, I've enjoyed getting to know folks."

"Folks like Walker?"

Her response was inaudible.

"Pardon?"

"I don't know," she said quietly.

Cord cleared his throat. "I thought maybe you and the girls might want to do a little exploring this afternoon."

Alda's head popped up.

"That's Courthouse Rock in the distance. If we find someone to lead the rest of the mules, we can take Bessie and ride ahead of the wagons. Providing it's fine with the MacDarbys."

"Could we, Miss Alda?" Pearl asked, wriggling in the saddle while her sister clutched her waist to keep from falling off the mule. "I'm sure Mamma will let us."

"Mamma says we need more exercise so we're tuckered out at night," Ruby said.

Alda stared toward the rock looming in the distance. "It would be a nice change, thank you. I'll ask the Henrys if maybe I can tie the mules to their wagon for the afternoon. I'll water them well, and they shouldn't give them any trouble."

"Go ahead and water the mules. You girls will help, won't you?"

The girls' bonnets bobbed like colorful birds.

"I'll speak to the MacDarbys and find someone to mind the mules."

"All right."

Bridget and Grey were more than willing to let the girls explore with Cord and Alda for the afternoon. Bridget packed some biscuits, jam, and jerky for the four of them and said she would look for the party to catch up after they made camp for the evening. She also said something about it being nice that Cord and Alda were having the opportunity to spend some time together. Bridget had blushed when Cord said he guessed they should if they were going to be married and all.

Cord steered Boss toward the men driving the cattle. The multi-colored herd of Texas Longhorns belonged to the Jacobs family. They'd sold three quarters of the herd with their ranch and planned to expand the herd again when they reached the new homestead in Oregon. Matthias Jacobs broke his leg when his horse stumbled in a prairie dog hole on the third day out. Most of the men took turns driving cattle and would until Matthias was healed well enough to get back on his horse.

The Jacobs had kept the best of the herd, and the animals were quiet. The trick was dodging their horns. Walker, Silas, and Neals Murch were driving the herd today.

Cord pressed Boss into a gallop and caught up with Walker. "Morning, Walker. Another fine day, wouldn't you say?"

"Sure, Cord, I'll give you that. It's a fine day. I know you didn't come all the way out here to talk about the weather. What can I do for you?"

"Miss Alda's thinking she needs a change of pace today and wants to take the girls exploring on Courthouse Rock."

Walker perked up in the saddle. "I'd be happy to accompany her and the girls. She send you out here to ask me?"

Cord pushed away the guilt he felt looking at Walker's hopeful face. "Nope. She wanted me to ask if you would watch her mules." *Forgive me, Lord.* "We all know how much you love those animals. The constant care you've been showing them…" Cord turned his head from side to side slowly, "it says a lot about a man."

Walker gazed toward Alda and the girls watering the mules with buckets. "You're sure she asked me to watch the mules and not go with her?"

"I said I'd come and talk to you."

Walker slumped in the saddle. "Tell her I'll be happy to watch the mules. Neals and Pa will be fine on their own. I'll let Pa know and be over shortly."

"Alda will appreciate it."

Boss's hooves formed dusty clouds as he rode toward Alda and the twins. *Lord, I'm sorry. I know I shouldn't have done it, but the boy was getting too big for his britches.* Walker was going to be mad as hops when he found out he'd been had.

And, Lord, I still need to know your will regarding Alda, or should I take the child's proclamation as your plan? Probably not; he and Alda had a lot to work out before there could be any talk of marriage.

Cord pulled on Boss's reins to bring him to a stop. The girls' dresses were soaked and dripping. The two giggled as they splashed each other with water from a bucket on the ground.

Bessie watched with her ears back as though waiting

for them to quit fooling around.

Alda's bonnet was pushed back on her shoulders, and tiny red ringlets stuck to the moisture on her forehead. It was a picture he would tuck away in his mind for the future.

Alda brushed the hair off her forehead and lifted a bucket to Bud's snout. "Girls, water that mule and stop wasting."

Cord chuckled as he jumped from Boss and swung down to retrieve the bucket the girls were playing in and watered Bessie. "I thought you girls were supposed to be helping."

Alda put her hands on her hips and faced them. "I thought so, too."

The girls ran over to Alda and looped their arms around her hips.

"We're sorry. We tried our best, but the water kept splashing us," Pearl said.

Alda laughed as she wrapped her arms around the girls and pulled them in tight. "I'll have to get after that water."

"Walker said he would care for the mules while we're exploring this afternoon."

"He did?" Alda tipped her head. "He said he wouldn't mind?" She released the girls, and they ran over to tuck their noses in some purple flowers growing alongside the road.

Cord looked down at the ground and nodded. "He said he'd be over shortly."

"I guess I'll untie Bessie then." Alda began to untie Moses's lead from the back of Bessie's saddle. "She'll enjoy being able to stretch her legs. I sure appreciate you taking the time to show the girls and me the rock. It would be a real shame to ride right by it and not get a chance to see it up close."

Sweat dotted Cord's neck. This was much harder than he thought it would be. Walker had left the cattle and was making his way toward them. "We should get moving. I'll take Ruby with me, and you can take Pearl. The mules should be fine. Walker's on his way."

Alda looked up and across Bessie's hind end. She waved to Walker, and he waved back.

"Mighty kind of him," she said.

Cord dismounted from Boss and lifted one of the twins onto each animal. They needed to get a move on before Walker reached them. "You ready?"

"I suppose. You're sure Walker's fine with this?"

"Yeah, he's fine." They both mounted their animals behind the girls, and Cord spurred Boss into a gallop. He looked over his shoulder. Alda rode behind them with a look of pure determination on her face. He'd been counting on the fact that she'd try and best him, even if there was no way her mule stood a chance.

Half an hour brought them within a stone's throw of the two towers.

Alda tipped her head back to take in the three hundred foot high Courthouse. "I never expected it to be this tall close up. You can't tell from a distance there are two. What's the shorter tower called?"

"The Jailhouse."

"Of course."

"It's a tough climb. We don't have to go all the way to the top, but even just a ways gives a nice view."

"Could we, Miss Alda?" Pearl asked.

"Are you sure your little legs can handle it?"

"Yes!" both girls replied.

Cord led them to a shaded nook where they could tie the animals. The four dismounted, and the girls scampered up the narrow trail skirted with sagebrush and yucca plants.

"Mind you don't hurt yourselves on those sharp leaves," Alda said.

The girls slowed for a moment and then dashed further up the trail.

"I don't know how Bridget does it. The girls have exhausted me after one morning."

Cord gestured with his arm for Alda to precede him up the trail. She lifted and wrapped the material of her riding skirt to keep it from tangling in the low lying brambles.

"Probably makes it easier if they're your own."

"Maybe."

Alda looked good following the steep trail. She had a grace about her steps that belied the difficulty of the terrain. "You're good with them, you know."

"I don't know about that. I'm just happy to be of some help to Bridget."

"No, really, and it's easy to see those girls adore you."

Alda halted and turned to face him. Standing uphill her green eyes almost looked him straight across. "Why, thank you, Mr. Cord," she said.

Cord swallowed. "I thought I told you the first day we met I didn't stand much on formality." His fingers fiddled with the dried bits of sagebrush he'd picked up along the trail.

"You surely did," her voice dropped to a whisper, "Cord."

Her eyes drew him in even further. Cord lifted his hat from his head and leaned forward to touch his lips against hers. Soft as flower petals, like he'd imagined.

"Miss Alda?"

Cord stepped back quickly and replaced his hat. A line of crimson rushed up Alda's face and disappeared into her beautiful curls. She turned toward the girls.

"Pearl cut her hand," Ruby said. Her little face was scrunched up like she was about to cry.

Alda toyed with the collar of her dress as she replied. "Can you show me where she is?" She took Ruby by the hand to lead her up the trail and around a precipice.

Pearl sat on the chalky ground one palm clasped against the other. Blood seeped around the edges of her tiny hands.

Alda knelt on the ground and took Pearl's hands in her own.

"I didn't listen. I wanted to see how sharp the leaves were so I grabbed one."

"Shhh, it's not your fault. I should have been paying closer attention."

Yup, they should have. It was his fault, too.

"Let me see."

Pearl gradually opened her hand revealing a narrow cut the length of her palm.

"Is she going to be all right? Mamma won't be happy if we take her back hurt."

"It's not deep, but it probably stings."

Pearl nodded her head.

"Mr. Cord, can we borrow your neckerchief?"

"It's none too clean. Probably not the best — "

Alda silenced him with a glare.

"Sure, you can borrow my bandana." He untied the knot at his neck.

Alda wiped Pearl's palm with her petticoat and wrapped it with his neckerchief. "You hold this tight, and I think it will stop bleeding shortly." She lifted Pearl from the ground and dusted the backside of her dress. "You girls stay close by so we don't have another incident."

Probably not another kiss either. He would have felt guiltier about the first one if he had planned it.

They followed the trail for another hundred and fifty feet before coming to a narrow cliff. He helped the others scramble over the rocks and up onto the overhang. Both Alda and Cord held the girls' hands.

"Beautiful, it's like you can see to the other side of the world." Alda pointed into the distance. "Look girls, over there; that's our wagon train."

Cord pointed out a golden eagle soaring above Jailhouse Rock.

The girls squealed and ducked as wrens flitted in and

out of the small crevices above their heads.

Cord looked over at Alda. It was the most perfect day he'd experienced in a long time.

Chapter Ten

Alda handed over the sleeping form of Pearl to her mother.

"Looks like someone finally managed to do what I've been trying to do since we left home. Did you drug these girls with something?"

Alda laughed. "No, it was a bit of a climb. The neckerchief is because she cut her hand. It's not deep, but you should put some salve on it in the morning."

Cord walked over with Ruby, and Grey lifted the girl from his arms.

"You two have a nice picnic?" Grey asked.

"Yes," Alda said. "But we're sorry Pearl hurt her hand."

She glanced over at Cord. He looked about as unsure as she felt. Where had that kiss come from? But she had to admit, the sun, the open sky, a beautiful backdrop to such a special moment. Cord wasn't making it easy to keep her distance.

"You folks have a good night. Alda, can I see you safe to your lodgings?" Cord asked.

"Thanks for letting us borrow the girls," Alda said as she rubbed small circles on Pearl's back. "Goodnight."

"See you in the morning," Bridget said.

Alda turned from the MacDarbys' wagon. Cord took her arm right above the elbow and directed her toward her tent on the inside of the circle next to Reverend and Mrs.

Heaton's wagon. She'd taken to erecting her tent next to the Heaton's when Walker had become more and more of a nuisance in his pursuit of her attentions. Next to a minister's wagon was the most modest location she could think of. It had cut down on Walker's late night attempts to engage her in meaningless conversation about the next day's travel.

Cord stopped shy of her tent and drew her around to face him. "I want to apologize for earlier today — "

One of Mr. Heaton's snores reverberated from inside the wagon, and Alda couldn't resist the urge to giggle. The man's knowledge of the scriptures had proved invaluable, but the sound of his snoring was almost enough to put her over the edge.

"I'm happy you find the situation amusing."

Alda reached out and touched the cotton sleeve of Cord's shirt. "I'm sorry, it's not you," she giggled again, "it's the snoring. I try to fall asleep to his cacophony every night. That, and maybe I'm a little bit nervous."

"Nervous? About what?"

Alda looked down at the ground. "About what you're going to say next."

"Well, if it isn't our two most ardent adventurers." Walker's voice held a hint of mockery.

Cord took a step back, and her hand dropped from his arm. He turned to face Walker.

Walker scowled back at Cord. "The whole train was taking bets on whether you folks would come back engaged after your ruse."

"Ruse? What are you talking about, Walker?" Alda asked.

"Your problem is with me. Leave Alda out of this."

"What's he talking about, Cord? And why would the train be taking bets? We hardly know each other."

Cord looked like she'd punched him in the stomach. "Walker and I are going to go and have a conversation.

We'll see you in the morning."

"I think she can hear what you have to say."

"Like I said, this is between me and you." Cord grabbed the younger man by the bicep and pulled him away from Alda. "We'll see you in the morning, Alda," he said over his shoulder.

Walker shook off Cord's grip and mumbled under his breath as the two men walked across the sand.

Alda watched their backs until they disappeared into the black of the night. If only Cord had had a chance to speak his mind before they were interrupted. She would have to seek him out tomorrow and find an opportunity to speak privately.

The next morning Alda winced as she climbed from her bedroll at the sound of the horn.

The muscles in her legs hurt more than she expected from their ascent the day before. She ran her tongue over her lips. The memory of Cord's sweet kiss was still vivid. All the tossing and turning of the night before hadn't solved the dilemma of Cord.

She liked him—maybe she was even growing to love him—but he loved the Lord, too. She didn't know if she ever fully could. The scriptures the Reverend had shared over meals gave her a lot to think about, but she still wasn't convinced she could love a God who appeared so distant, so uninvolved.

Alda dressed and ran a comb through her curls before going to join the others for breakfast. Bridget and the girls were eating oatmeal with the others around the fire. Mrs. Jacobs offered her a bowl, and Alda thanked her for it then sat down on a blanket by Bridget. She glanced over the other folks slurping coffee and eating their breakfasts. Walker nodded when her eyes met his, and then he resumed talking with Mr. Pickett.

Where was Cord? Maybe he was helping drive cattle today. She looked toward the herd but couldn't see his tall form on Boss. "Bridget, have you seen Cord this morning?"

Bridget's pretty eyebrows pulled together. "He didn't come and talk to you?"

"No, why?"

"He told Grey he had some business to attend to in Sidney. Grey told him he should let you know as he figured you'd be looking for him today."

"Because …"

"Ruby told us about the kiss." Bridget's contagious laughter resonated from her chest, and several people turned at the sound of it.

Alda lifted a hand to shade her eyes and whispered to Bridget, "Can you please not mention it?"

So Ruby had noticed. Bridget and Grey probably thought Alda and Cord were completely irresponsible — maybe they were.

Bridget put her arm around Alda and brought her lips close to her ear. "Don't worry; I don't plan to announce it. I did my best to convince Ruby you would be mad at her and wouldn't take her on any more adventures if she told anyone else. Time will tell." Bridget released Alda's shoulders and took another spoonful of oatmeal.

"So Cord didn't mention he was leaving for a few days?"

"A few days? Did he say why?"

"No, he didn't give any other details. He hopes to meet up with us in Cheyenne. Grey told the others we would keep an eye on you, although Walker was more than willing — speak of the devil."

Walker had left the group of men discussing plans for the day's travels and moseyed over to where the two women were seated.

"I'm going to finish up the last of my packing." Bridget rose from the blanket. "Good morning, Mr. Parsons." She said before urging the girls toward their wagon.

Walker plopped down on the blanket in her place.

Alda gathered the edges of her skirt and tucked them under her legs leaving a gap between them.

"Don't worry, I won't bite, although I don't know if I can say the same for a certain other gentleman."

"Walker, I'm not in the mood to be bothered this morning. I need to go and see to my packing as well." Alda attempted to rise from the horse blanket. Walker reached over to grip her wrist and pulled her back down. "What are you doing?" she said, circling the spot with her fingers where her wrist stung.

"I heard Mr. Cord up and left for a few days."

"Did you have anything to do with it?"

"No, but I don't mind." He leaned closer. "It gives us more of an opportunity to spend time together."

Walker's pushy manner had grown irksome. Cord was so many things Walker wasn't and most likely would never be. "We won't be spending any time together."

Walker straightened his spine, and his eyes took on a look of stone as he snarled under his breath. "I can assure you we will."

Alda skimmed the others to see if anyone else was watching them. They all seemed to be preoccupied with breakfast or conversation. What was Walker inferring? She had no intention of spending time with him. She sucked in a quick breath. "Mr. Parsons, you're being ill-mannered. I don't wish to have any further discussion with you. Don't try and prevent me from leaving again, or I will raise my voice and let everyone know what you are up to."

Walker sniggered and lifted his palms in the air. "Until later then, Miss Alda."

~

Cord slowed Boss to a walk. "You definitely earned your keep today, boy. Sorry I had to drive you so hard."

A long day's ride south through scattered farms nestled in the rough scrub of ranch land brought Cord and Boss within sight of the town of Sidney. He'd hated not telling

Alda he was leaving for a couple of days, but departing at four in the morning did not make for good timing to share his plans with her. Grey had been watching the cattle when he left, and Cord told him he had business in town and nothing else.

Cord rubbed the week's worth of beard on his chin. With that and remaining inconspicuous, he hoped no one would recognize him. He hadn't been stationed in Sidney, but occasionally army business sent him to the fort. He hadn't been back since he'd requested military discharge two years before.

Folks were saying the town had cleaned up a lot, mostly because of the fiasco, which saw poor Jack McDonald contorting on the wrong end of a rope for over fifteen minutes. The man was a criminal, sure, but nobody deserved to die that way. Word had gotten out the same thing would happen to any other unsavory creatures who didn't hightail it out of town. The low numbers milling about on Front Street indicated the citizens had taken the threat seriously.

Two years ago, the place was crawling with brothels and saloons. It brought a smile to his face to see quite a few boarded up and others hanging out a different shingle.

The dry goods store on the corner was as good a place as any to water Boss and let him rest. A whole lot of listening and people watching at a few strategic locations, and Cord should know if Doc Rufus and his sons were in town or not.

The hunch had struck him about midnight last night. He'd gone from pondering what possessed him to kiss Alda so forthrightly to figuring out there was a hint of a pattern to the gang's whereabouts.

The three had crisscrossed from Wyoming to Nebraska and back to Wyoming several times and usually hit a train on the outskirts of a town. If they were headed back to Wyoming after the botched job near Kearney, no one would suspect them of hiding out in a town with such a strong military presence.

The gang was bold, and Doc's boys were arrogant. Their get-ups on the poster told him that. It would be just like them to hole up in a town known for dealing harsh judgments on its lawbreakers.

Over an hour later, Cord took another sip from the one glass of whiskey he'd been nursing in Tobin's Bar. The drink was like fire in his throat. He'd never developed a taste for the stuff. He leaned back in his chair and pulled his hat low over his eyes. Maybe the nosey bartender giving him a sideways glance would figure he was sleeping. The warmth of the body-filled room caused his eyelids to droop. He rubbed down the sides of both cheeks to wake up.

For two hours, the chatter around him was the usual male bravado, and not a single word about Doc or his sons.

Cord waited for another half hour before nodding to the bartender and making his exit through the double doors.

Half a dozen men and two soldiers in full dress loitered on the corner of the boardwalk. Cord lifted a hand to the brim of his hat and twisted on one boot to head the other direction.

"Preston, is that you?"

Levi Hull. Cord should have known he couldn't get in and out of Sidney without being recognized. He didn't know the young soldier well, but he knew he was bright. Levi had carried several messages to various posts for Cord in the past. Keep walking; don't turn around.

"You, there!" Levi hollered at his back. "Hold up."

It would bring too much attention to him if he didn't stop. Cord slowed and then turned around. "Me?" he said meeting Levi's eyes. "Were you meaning me, Sir?"

"I — "

"You must be mistaken, Sir. The name's Cord."

Levi's curious look held Cord's gaze as he replied.

"Sorry, you looked like someone I know."

Cord nodded to Levi and the other curious faces now taking him in. "If you don't mind, Sir, I'll be on my way."

Levi nodded back, "Proceed."

Cord took three long steps before letting out the breath he was holding and twisting his neck to relieve the build-up of tension. *Thanks, Levi.* No doubt the boy would be seeking him out later to ask him a few questions. With any luck, the whole thing would explain itself.

One block down, he ducked into the Metropolitan Hotel and through the swinging doors labeled "Gentlemen Only." It would take some doing to find an actual gentleman in Sidney.

Cord kept his head down as he elbowed his way to the polished bar mumbling "'scuse me" several times under his breath. The crowd pressed even tighter around the piano where a woman dressed in a low cut, blue gown and a ridiculous feathered hat sat playing and crooning her way through "Golden Slippers."

He ordered another whiskey from one of the men hustling to serve customers and leaned on the counter. Maybe it would be his last drink of the night. With the throng of patrons in the place, no one would notice how long it took him to down it.

A raw-boned fellow with his greasy, brown hair pulled back into a tail plunked Cord's drink within inches of his elbow. Liquid spilled over the side and formed a puddle.

"Sorry 'bout that," the bartender said as he lifted the whiskey to swipe under it with the white cloth in his other hand. "I can top it up for you."

Cord held a palm up. "No need," he said and slid a fifty cent piece across the bar.

The man raised one eyebrow. "All right," he said, returning Cord's glass.

Cord took the drink and turned to roam through the crowd. A steady stream of men wandered in. Word must have spread about the concert. The high notes the woman was hitting — enough to set a man's teeth on edge — were probably the reason for the steady stream of men heading out the door just as fast.

Cord braced himself against the far wall and across from the swinging doors to take advantage of the traffic.

The entertainer moved on to a rousing version of "Polly Wolly Doodle," and the crowd commenced rocking from shoulder to shoulder with their drinks held aloft. Many of the drinks were sloshing over the sides of the glasses and landing on neighbors' sleeves.

The night could prove to be a long one.

Around one a.m., Cord found himself wondering if Aggie Dear's voice would ever give out. She'd introduced herself as such several times during the night's entertainment. The crowd showed no signs of waning either. With the number of men coming and going, the entire town must have circulated through at least once. He lifted his hat and ran his fingernails back along his scalp to wake himself up. Loud ruckus or not, he couldn't stay awake much longer; he would have to take a room down the block and get some shut-eye. Maybe he'd been way off in his figuring, and Doc hadn't been thinking bold at all.

Cord shifted, putting his other shoulder against the wall. His eye caught the features of a tall, dark haired, young man coming through the door. The man pulled the collar of his oilskin up and glanced quickly around the room. There was something familiar about the boy's face, but the hair color wasn't right. If it was one of Doc's sons, he'd lost a considerable amount of weight.

The young man pushed his way closer to the piano, and Cord followed. When they stopped, Cord could count the moles on the back of the kid's neck, he was so close. How the boy could keep the heavy coat on in the heat of the room was a mystery.

"A bit warm for a jacket like that," he said into the

kid's ear.

At Cord's words, the kid started — elbowing his neighbor in the process.

"Watch what you're doing," the man said, displaying a mouthful of wax-yellow teeth.

Cord grabbed the kid by the arm. "Don't mind my friend here. He's getting over excited. He hasn't heard singing this fine in a long time."

The neighbor glanced at the boy and grinned before rejoining the tenth or eleventh round of "Oh Ain't I Got the Blues."

The kid tried to wrestle his arm out of Cord's grip. "Let go of me," he said through gritted teeth.

An innocent man would have made a scene. Cord leaned toward the boy's ear once more, "Sure I will, if you tell me your name's not Owen or Emmet."

The boy froze.

Crack. Something hit Cord's kneecap — hard — his fingers lost their grip on the boy as he doubled over. "Uuuugh," Cord said before clamping his jaw to keep from yelling out again.

"You feeling all right, Mister?" someone asked.

"Yup." Cord managed to squeak out. He drew in a few ragged breaths before running his hand over his knee. It didn't feel broken, but it hurt like the devil. He sucked in another couple of breaths. He should have seen it coming. The kid must have had a length of pipe or something in his pocket. Cord tensed his stomach and righted himself.

The kid had slipped through the crowd. He was gone.

Cord took a tentative step, and the pain shot clear through to his toes. He waited a few minutes before limping toward the salon doors and out onto the boardwalk. A weathered bench sat against the hotel wall, and Cord lowered himself onto it. He had to give it to Doc; he'd trained his boys well.

There was no way he could pursue the kid. Cord's knee

would be out of commission for a couple of days at least. He should hobble his way to the fort and have them be on the lookout for Doc and his boys, but they were probably already on their way out of town. He might as well get a room. Cord braced himself and rose from the bench. He took several painful steps down the sidewalk and rounded the corner. As he crossed the alley, two figures stepped out of the darkness.

"Any chance you are looking for this fellow?" Levi asked. He was wearing civilian dress. With one hand, he pushed the kid in front of him. He lifted a pistol and chunk of pipe with the other hand. "He was packing these; tried to use the pipe on me, too. I guess the element of surprise was gone. He's fast though, I'll give him that."

The kid's hands were tied behind his back, and blood streamed from his nose and down onto the collar of his coat. He looked at Cord and spit on the dirt. The bloody sputum landed within inches of Cord's boot.

"How'd you know to grab him?"

"I figured you had a good reason for not wanting anyone to know who you were, and I thought maybe you could use some assistance. My vantage point wasn't as good as yours, but I've been enjoying the show about as long as you have." Levi smirked. "This boy owes us. Who is he?"

"I'm pretty sure he's one of Doc Rufus's boys."

Levi jerked his head back; his eyes stretched open. "*The* Doc Rufus? The same one we've been looking for high and low for weeks now?"

Cord glanced at the kid — not a muscle on his face moved. "Where are your pa and your brother?" he asked.

The kid didn't say a word; his face was a mask as he stared off across the street.

"Well, he's not denying anything, and that can be as good as an answer. I'm in no shape to take him in though. Could you deliver him to the sheriff? Maybe he can get him to talk."

"I'd be delighted." Levi snugged his grip on the kid's arm.

"I'm going to take a room at Chowin's. Come and find me there in the morning."

"Let's go," Levi said, dragging his captive with him. "I'll see you on the morrow, Pres — I mean Cord."

Cord dipped his head. "I appreciate it."

Cord stumbled another block and paid a heavy-eyed clerk for a room. His boots had barely hit the floor beside the bed when sleep overtook him.

A persistent knock on the door woke him the next morning.

"Give me a minute," he mumbled and rubbed his eyes to clear the cobwebs.

"Cord, it's me, Levi."

Cord fell forward and caught himself on the washbasin when he attempted to stand. His knee sported a large lump on one side and throbbed like someone was trying to hammer clean through it. He shuffled two steps to the door and turned the key in the lock.

Levi entered and dropped a white envelope on the table under the window.

"Take a seat," Cord said, indicating one of the black wooden chairs next to the table.

"How's the knee?" Levi asked.

"The kid got me good." Cord said, clenching his jaw to take another few steps to the other chair, and sat down. "Ever get a name out of him?" Cord unbuttoned the wrist of his cotton sleeve and commenced folding the material up to his elbow.

"Nope, the sheriff didn't get anything useful, and now he won't."

Cord paused his folding and looked at Levi whose mouth stretched in a grim line. "Why's that?"

"He downed some sort of poison shortly after I took

him in."

"Huh?"

"I went back to the barracks to get some sleep. One of the deputies came by this morning with the envelope. He said the kid asked for a glass of water shortly after I left. He must have slipped a pill or something into his mouth while they weren't looking. A few minutes later, he was grabbing his stomach and screaming. A couple of minutes after that, he was fighting for breath. The deputy's hands shook as he told me the story. Hard to believe a father would ask that of his son."

"The sheriff figures he's one of Doc Rufus's sons then?"

"Yup, says there's no question."

Lord, have mercy on the poor boy's soul.

"Deputy gave me this." Levi lifted the envelope and tapped the edge on the table as he spoke. "As the posters say, 'dead or alive.'"

Cord's gut rolled at the remark. He was part of the reason the kid was dead.

"I didn't tell him I was coming to you, and I don't think anyone else saw us talking last night. Is this how you make a living now, bounty hunting?"

Cord reached for the envelope and slid his finger under the flap. He fanned the five, crisp, one hundred dollar bills on the table. "I figure we should split this."

Levi gaped at the money on the table and reached forward to slide his fingers down several of the bills. "I don't believe I've seen this much money all in one place. It's over a year's worth of wages, but I don't expect you to pay me."

Cord put an index finger on a bill and pushed it toward Levi. "You earned it," he said and pushed another bill across the table. "I wasn't going to catch him after he smashed my knee."

"I had no clue what I was doing."

Cord plucked the other three bills from the table. "That makes two of us."

Chapter Eleven

The soaring, snow-capped Rocky Mountains painted a welcome background after two days of rolling hills covered with dense patches of prickly pear. Alda pondered on the verses Pastor Heaton had shared in a short service the day before.

"But thou, O Lord, art a God full of compassion, and gracious, longsuffering, and plenteous in mercy and truth."

Such a contrast from her pa, whose patience ran about as long as his arm. And if a lie would suit a situation better, he would gladly leave the truth behind.

Her favorite scripture portion so far was, "That you, being rooted and grounded in love, may be able to comprehend with all the saints what is the breadth and length and height and depth …"

If only she could experience a love like that — Alda looked up at the white peaks soaring into the blue sky — love so large, you couldn't see the end of it. Her heart surged within her chest. Maybe she could know a love like that.

The wagon train had overnighted at the Pine Bluffs Railroad Station the night before and had filled their barrels from the tall water tank along the tracks. Walker had come by twice last evening to insist on a visit. The first time she rebuffed him, he stalked off down the tracks, smacking his cowboy hat against his leg and arguing with himself. The second time he came around, Pastor Heaton gave him a thorough tongue lashing and told him if he didn't stop bothering her, he would have to speak to his father.

Walker had directed several black looks her way at lunchtime, but he didn't bother to try and speak to her again. Alda couldn't quite put her finger on what didn't feel right about him.

The mules would enjoy the two days' rest the wagon train planned to spend in Cheyenne before going over the pass, although over the last couple of days the roads were the best they'd seen since leaving home.

Alda twisted on Bessie's back and looked out onto the horizon. The corners of her mouth turned up into a smile at the familiar shape on the grey horse. Cord was back.

Alda couldn't tame the thumping of her heart when Cord drew up alongside Bessie.

"Evening, Miss Alda," he said lifting the black Stetson a few inches from his head and then returning it.

"Evening, Mr. Cord." Alda looked over and fluttered her eyelashes. *Shameless*, her pa would have said. Maybe it was, but who cared; Cord's bulging eyes made the flirtation worth it.

He cleared his throat. "You got something in your eye?"

Funny. Alda kicked Bessie with her heels, and the pack string picked up the pace.

"Alda, slow down. I'm sorry. I just didn't expect it."

Alda pulled on the reins, and Bessie relaxed her stride. "Didn't expect what, Mr. Cord?"

Cord's face split into a wide grin. "That you would miss me so much."

He'd taken the teasing too far. Never mind that her romance skills were apparently deplorable. She hadn't decided if they were even suited for one another *yet*. Alda nudged Bessie into a trot, and her gear rattled in the packs. Cord's elated laughter trailed at her back.

"Would you please slow down? My knee's pounding

something fierce. You know I'm just fooling with you."

Sure, she knew, but it was nice to hear him admit it. Alda tugged Bessie back into a walk. "What happened to your knee?"

"You could say it was a casualty of my occupation."

"So you did go to Sidney for bounty hunting. I wish you'd told me."

Cord's dark eyes sought hers and held. "Why?" he asked gently.

Why? Because she cared if he was in danger, because he was important to her, because … she was growing fond of him. "I want to know, that's all. I'm the only one here you've told what you do for a living. What if you went missing or something?"

"I imagine it would be too late."

"Wh- what are you saying?"

"It's the nature of the job: injuries, danger, death."

"Death? Your death? But I thought — "

"Like I said before, the criminal elements don't take kindly to being rounded up. One of Doc Rufus's boys cracked me on the knee."

"So you found them, Doc Rufus and his boys?" Alda's voice carried her excitement. "They won't be holding up any more trains or killing any more women and children?"

"I found one of the boys. I don't even know if it was Emmet or Owen."

"It's just a matter of time then, isn't it, until the boy reveals where the others are?"

"Afraid not. He killed himself while in custody; used one of his pa's concoctions, most likely. The deputy said it was a horrible death."

What could she say? Alda grieved the choices that would bring a young man to such a violent end. And yet she was glad he wouldn't be able to hurt anyone else again, including Cord.

Several minutes passed without conversation.

"A life with someone like me would hold many days of uncertainty."

Alda's gaze searched the nearest peak. "Uncertainty, Mr. Cord, is one thing we can all count on."

Two hours later, whoops and shouts from Silas brought men and women running. The group had set up camp beside a large, placid lake surrounded by foothills loaded with lofty pines and trembling aspens. Alda looked up from brushing Jenny, and her stomach sank. Fifty yards behind Silas, Walker, riding on Prince, held the reins leading Boss. Cord hung over Boss's saddle and his arms swayed back and forth with the movement of the horse.

Alda dropped the brush and ran with the others.

"Miss Alda, go back to camp," Silas said as she neared. "Let the rest of us look after him."

Alda kept running.

Mr. Murch and Grey untied the ropes binding Cord to Boss and carefully slid him to the ground. Boss's side was soaked with blood; small red droplets fell and dotted the grass near Cord's form.

Alda covered her mouth to keep from retching as she knelt on the ground next to Cord. "Is he alive?" she asked.

Grey pressed his fingers on the underside of Cord's wrist. "He's alive. What happened, Walker?"

Walker took a step back. "Now don't go blaming me. I had no idea that cow was going to turn on him. One minute he and Boss were pushing her out of the thicket toward the others, and the next minute he was howling at me to come and help him."

Alda looked over at Walker who was staring at the ground. *Look up, Walker, so I can see if you are telling the truth.*

"I did the best I could. He's lost a lot of blood, though. He passed out about a mile from here."

Grey untied the knot of Cord's sleeve which had been wound and tied around his leg. His jeans were torn from the upper thigh to right above the knee. A deep gash in the muscle of his thigh steadily oozed red onto his blood soaked pant leg. A slip of bone showed in the middle of the wound.

Alda squeezed her eyes shut.

The men and women around her hushed.

Cord groaned and then coughed but didn't regain consciousness.

Alda opened her eyes. "Can we find a doctor? There must be a doctor in Cheyenne." She took Cord's hand in her own and pressed. "Cord, please, wake up," she said willing him to respond. "Grey, can we get a doctor? Please, he needs to see a doctor!"

Grey looked over at Silas who gave a faint shake of his head.

An arm went around her shoulders.

"Alda," Bridget said, "come with me." She tugged at Alda's fingers attempting to peel them from around Cord's hand.

"I'm not going anywhere," Alda's voice hitched. "We need to get him to a doctor."

Bridget dropped her hand, placing it on the center of Alda's back. "Alda," she said quietly, "let the men help him."

"Grey," Alda begged. "Grey, please," she sobbed, "take him to a doctor."

Grey raised his hands to his hips and scanned the faces of the men and women circled around Cord. "Everett and Archie, go and empty the Jacobs' second wagon," he said. "Martha, find some blankets to keep Cord comfortable in the wagon. Joshua, you and I will patch him up as best we can and take him into Cheyenne." His gaze dropped to Alda. "Go back with Bridget and pray; pray like you've never prayed before."

"Thank you," she said touching the top of Grey's boot. "Thank you."

Bridget helped her up from the ground and pulled her away from the group.

They were half way back to camp when Alda spoke, "I hate him."

"Hate who?"

"Walker," Alda stomped the heels of her boots into the dirt. "I know he had something to do with this."

"You don't," Bridget said. "You don't know anything for sure."

"I know he was angry when I wouldn't give my attention, and I know he was angry when Cord and I took the girls to the rocks the other day."

"That doesn't prove anything."

Alda stopped and covered her face with her hands. "But what if Cord dies?" Her shoulders quaked. "I should have known Walker could be dangerous. I should have warned Cord when Walker asked him to help find the missing longhorns."

Bridget wrapped her arms around Alda's shoulders and pulled her close. "Blaming yourself or Walker won't help Cord right now. Like Grey said, you need to pray."

If only she knew how.

That night, Alda lay stretched out on her bedroll fully dressed. The orb of the moon glowed through the canvas of her tent.

The wagon, with Cord still unconscious, had rolled out of camp over two hours ago. She had yet to utter a single word in prayer. Cord deserved an effort. He'd said in the chophouse that Jesus wasn't like her pa, that Jesus *would never leave you or forsake you.* Pastor Heaton had said the same thing. If God wouldn't abandon Cord, she could talk to God on Cord's behalf.

Alda exhaled a long breath. "God, You don't know me, but this is Alda. I want to talk to You about Cord. He knows You, and he's a good man. Right now, he needs Your help. Pastor Heaton said there wasn't a single thing in the whole world that could separate people from Your love."

Alda nibbled the corner of her lip.

"He's hurt, Lord. He's really hurt. Please help him."

Alda turned over on her side and curled up into a ball. Her eyelids fluttered closed.

Mid-morning the next day, the mules munched their grain while Alda finished brushing out their coats. Ruby and Pearl scampered around gathering wildflowers and giggled when the animals nibbled them from their palms.

How wonderful it would be to not have a care in the world.

Grey hadn't returned with Cord. It was probably a good sign. If Cord had died, he would have — she pushed the thought from her mind.

Right before noon, Grey and Joshua drove into camp with the wagon. Grey slid from the wagon seat and onto the ground before reaching over the sideboard and pulling out a patchwork quilt. He snapped it in the wind and put it over one arm before reaching in for another.

Cord wasn't in the wagon. The strength drained away from Alda's legs, and she crumpled to her knees on the ground. *Lord, I thought You would help him.*

Joshua jumped from the wagon and ran across the stretch of grass to Alda's side. "Cord's alive, Miss Alda. He's in rough shape, but he's alive." He bent forward and lifted Alda to her feet.

"Where is he?"

"We left him at the hospital. A doctor sewed him up, but he said Cord's loss of blood was critical. They're injecting him with saline; the doctor figures he'll pull through."

I'm sorry, Lord, for doubting that You cared about Cord. "Can I go and see him?"

"I can take you back to town tomorrow morning. He still hadn't regained consciousness before we left."

~

Neals and Martha Murch's oldest son Joshua brought the wagon to a halt in front of the Cheyenne County Hospital, a long, one-story building with a hip roof and wraparound porch in front of a two-story, brick building with a flat roof. Crews of men shoveled dirt and planted trees on the extensive grounds.

"The hospital opened a couple of months ago. Cord's in Ward Four, second floor of the two story. You'll have to watch out for the head nurse. She's a stickler for rules."

Alda rested her gloved hand on the front of the wagon. "Thank you for driving me in. I'm sure it was an inconvenience."

"Not really. Pa asked me to pick up some supplies and feed for the oxen while I'm in town. I'll come back in a couple of hours."

Alda descended from the wagon and followed the makeshift sidewalk to the two-story building. A brown set of double doors led to a square foyer with a wide staircase on the far wall. Her feet scuffed on the threshold as she stepped through the doorway, and the smell of disinfectant stung her nose.

A young nurse in a blue uniform with a crisp white apron sat writing at a desk beside the stairs.

She looked up as the door closed behind Alda. "May I help you?"

Alda clutched her gloved hands together and cleared her throat. "I'm here to visit Cord."

The woman leaned forward as though expecting more explanation.

Alda wrung her hands. Cord had never told her his last name or if Cord was even his real name. Grey and Joshua wouldn't have known any more than she did. "He was brought in yesterday afternoon. A longhorn gouged one of his legs."

"Ahh. You mean the tall fellow in Ward Four. Go up

the stairs to the second floor; it's on your right." The nurse tucked her chin down, the scratch of her pen signifying Alda's dismissal.

Alda passed the desk, lifted the edge of her skirt, and ascended the staircase. A narrow metal sign riveted to a wooden door indicated Ward Four. She turned the brass knob and pushed the door open a few inches. In the second bed down from the door, Cord's pale face lay atop a starched white pillow case.

Lord, thank you. Tears gathered behind her eyes as she watched the gentle rise and fall of Cord's chest under the grey blanket. *You did not desert him.*

And nor could she. Alda's heart pulsed with the love she could no longer deny —
the love for a man … and His God. A God who cared about His family, not like a fickle earthly father — like her own father — but a God whose love was deep and wide. Like Pastor Heaton shared, a Father who let His own innocent Son die a brutal death on a cross so that she could experience His love. "I *will* love You back," she whispered, and as Alda closed her eyes, her soul tumbled into the unfathomable love of her heavenly Father.

Alda pushed the door open a few more inches and stepped into the room. The latch snicked shut behind her. A potbellied stove in the center of the long, rectangular room warmed the air of the ward. Cord was the only patient in the room.

Alda carried a metal chair from behind the door over to the head of his bed and sat down. After removing her gloves, she took Cord's hand in hers. "Cord, how are you doing?"

His chest continued to rise and fall, but he did not respond.

He didn't look like the same man who'd helped with Bessie the first day they met. Or the same Man who'd come to her rescue when Felix attacked her. Or even the same man who'd kissed her on the heights of Courthouse Rock. He looked small — vulnerable.

Sweat plastered the hair to his brow. Alda drew the tips of her fingers across his forehead and pushed it to the side. The scar along the edge of his jaw looked angry against his whitewashed cheek. She followed the curve of it with her thumb.

"I don't know how I can be all you need in a wife or if you even want me," she whispered. "But I know one thing, I never want to be without you."

The door popped open, and a plump nurse bustled into the room.

Alda pulled her hand back from Cord's face.

The woman stopped, and her dark eyes narrowed when she noticed Alda. "Excuse me, Miss, did they not tell you this patient mustn't have any visitors?"

Why hadn't Joshua or the front desk mentioned it? "No."

"Are you his wife?" the nurse asked.

"No," Alda said, fiddling with the cuff of her sleeve.

"His betrothed?"

Alda stifled the high-pitched titter as best she could. "No."

"Family then?"

Alda sucked in her upper lip and shook her head.

"Then why ever," the nurse put her hands on her hips and huffed. "I will have to speak to that girl." She crossed to the end of Cord's bed and faced Alda. "You're going to have to leave immediately. The patient has not regained consciousness nor has the doctor determined the extent of his injuries."

Alda picked up her gloves from her lap and rose from the chair. "Will he be able to have visitors tomorrow?"

"Miss, we run a respectable hospital …"

What was the woman implying?

"If you are not family, I suggest you wait until the

patient is discharged."

Alda dropped her head and sniffed at the sting of the remark. "I'll be going now," she said, her skirt rustling in the speed of her exit.

Chapter Twelve

Cord thrashed his head from side to side to force back the blackness. Muffled voices mingled together and faded. Who were they? He coughed and struggled for air to fill his lungs.

"Mr. Cord, Mr. Cord, you're all right now," a voice said. Bands slipped over both his wrists. He yanked to free himself, but they wouldn't budge.

Something sharp pierced his upper arm. He twisted to draw away from the pain.

"Hold on, Mr. Cord. It's for your own good."

Cord coughed again. His eyes blinked open.

"Welcome back," said a man in a black suit coat — a stethoscope around his neck.

Cord's gaze flew around the room, taking in the rows of identical metal beds. A doctor was poking a large needle into his bicep. "I'm in the hospital?"

"Yes, you are," said the man. "And it's a good thing. You wouldn't have survived otherwise. I'm Dr. Cooper, and this is Nurse Harfield."

Cord took in the grim expression of the woman handing the doctor a second liquid filled needle to inject. "What's in the needles?"

"They're saline injections," Dr. Cooper said. "It's what brought you through the loss of blood. Your injury is healing well — no sign of infection."

Cord attempted to bend the knee of his bandaged leg.

The muscles screamed in retaliation. "Uuuggh," he groaned. "What's my injury?"

"You were gored by a longhorn. It tore through to the bone."

Must have been the longhorn caught in the brush. The last thing he remembered was Walker shooting his gun off.

The syringe clinked as the nurse returned it to a metal tray and picked up another one.

"Your leg will be out of commission for a while," Dr. Cooper said.

The needle descended once more to his upper arm, and Cord clenched his jaw as it poked beneath the surface. "How long have I been here?"

"Four days," said the nurse.

"Four days? I've been here for four days?" How was it even possible? He had no recollection at all.

"Yes, you're quite a miracle," the doctor said. "I'll leave you in nurse Harfield's capable hands and continue my rounds. You should be able to leave in the next week if your wound continues to heal well and you have someone to care for you. Good day." The doctor tugged the edges of his black coat together with both fists and turned from Cord's bed to leave the room.

Cord scrunched his eyebrows together. "Four days, are you sure?" he asked the nurse who'd finished the last of her needles and had begun smoothing the edges of the grey blanket on his bed.

"I know how to count, young man." The woman pulled the bottom corner of his blanket out and, with a quick hand, smoothed and tucked it under the mattress.

"Has anyone come to visit? A woman with red — "

"The doctor said only family."

Alda hadn't been to see him? Perhaps Walker was keeping her busy, the scoundrel. Cord couldn't prove it, but he was sure Walker had set off his gun intentionally. Cord had followed the cow into the trees on Walker's signal. Her horns had wedged between a couple of cottonwoods. He'd dismounted from Boss to pry her loose. It wouldn't have been a problem if Walker's gun hadn't gone off, startling the cow.

He'd have to rely on others for how he ended up in the hospital. "Is this Cheyenne?" he asked.

"Yes, you're at Cheyenne County Hospital. I'll go and see if I can find you some tea and toast. You won't be able to eat much more for a day or two." Nurse Harfield picked up her tray from the next bed and bustled out of the room.

Cord stared out the window across from his bed — blue sky and nothing else. He must be on the second story or higher. He ran his fingers around the knee without a bandage, the one Doc's son had hit. No lump — a good thing if his other one was laid up.

What had happened to the wagon train? Had they moved on and over the pass? He couldn't really blame them if they did. They knew he didn't have a destination in mind for himself. Grey and Bridget would look out for Alda.

He'd miss her though. His gut wrenched. Who was he kidding? He would miss her a whole lot. Cord pictured Alda's pretty face and bright smile. If only she were the one who would *care for him,* as the doc had said.

~

Alda sat stunned. Silas, Grey, Pastor Heaton, and Everett Woolsey all shifted uneasily on the crude benches they'd placed facing one another a hundred feet from the nearest wagon.

Silas continued his diatribe, "We don't want you to take it personal, Miss Lealand."

Alda's blood picked up its pace. "Not take it personal, Mr. Parsons? Which part shouldn't I take personal? The fact you're leaving him here in Cheyenne, or the fact that it's your son who put him in the hospital in the first place?"

"Now, now, Missy, there's no need for you to go smearing my son's good reputation."

Alda snorted. "If you think he has a good reputation, you're the only one around this circle who does."

Silas's eyes popped. "Just a minute," he said, his gaze darting from one man to the next, looking for someone to disagree.

"Silas, this ain't about Walker," Grey said.

Finally, some reason.

"Alda, we have to do what's best for the train. Waiting the last four days has put us behind."

"But — "

Grey put his palm up toward her. "Listen, none of us here want to move on without him."

Silas continued to sulk. Every other man nodded.

"We've got no choice. Joshua stopped in at the hospital the other day. They wouldn't let him see Cord, but the nurse said he needed another week, at least. Even then he won't be able to travel."

So what if the rest of them were willing to abandon Cord; she wasn't. "I'm not going with you."

"Alda, listen," Grey said. "I know you think you're doing the right thing. We understand, but we're asking you to reconsider. You wanted to get those mules to your uncle in California. We can help you do that before your money and supplies run out."

The others commenced bobbing their heads.

How could she explain? There wasn't a single reason the world over that would cause her to abandon Cord. The Lord wanted her to care for him, help him; she knew it in her heart. Since the morning in the hospital, she'd spent time every day in prayer for Cord, and for herself. The others could move on, but she wasn't going to. She'd have to find the means to stay, but surely something would present itself.

"I'm not going. You folks do what you need to do. No

hard feelings. The mules and I will be fine until Cord can travel. Then we will continue on our way."

Grey let out a slow breath. "Alda, we have no business telling you what to do. The train will be moving on in the morning. You still have time to reconsider."

Silas pushed his dumpy hat back on his greasy hair. "Well, I'm not giving either of them their money back," he said.

Grey raised his voice and pointed his finger. "Silas, you can give half their money back, and you can do it without whining."

Silas's face looked sheepish as he commenced muttering under his breath. The circle of men broke up, and Alda wandered back to her mules.

Alda lifted Bessie's forelock with one hand and dropped her forehead to meet the mule's.

"Bessie," she whispered, "I'm going to need your help with the others. It looks like it's you and me again, at least until Cord's out of the hospital.

She would have to find a way to sneak in and talk to Cord. Then she would know how much longer she would have to wait for sure.

Alda lifted her head and looked over at her tent. She'd probably be safe enough along the lake — alone. Maybe Cord could give her some advice on that, too.

~

Vivid oranges and purples broke across the morning sky as Silas whistled for the train to commence leaving. Walker hadn't been seen since the day Cord had been injured. Rumor had it his dad had sent him home. It was a good thing, too. Alda would've had a hard time controlling herself. He was guilty, and he needed to be taught a lesson.

Alda crossed the grass to Bridget and Grey's wagon. She rested a hand on the sidestep and looked up.

One tear coursed down Bridget's cheek. "I was wondering when you were going to come over and say goodbye," she said.

Alda dropped her chin down to her chest. She'd miss Bridget terribly. The woman had filled a part of the hole Mamma had left behind. And the girls, nothing would replace those two little darlings. "I'm not very good at goodbyes."

Bridget stood up in the wagon, wrapped her skirt around her legs, and jumped to the ground. The two women embraced one another in a tight hug.

"It's not too late. Grey and I could help you pack up, and then we could catch up with the rest," Bridget said.

Would it be a better idea? No, Cord needed her. Alda broke the embrace and swiped a tear from her own cheek. "I'll miss you folks. Maybe I can visit after I've delivered the pack string. If you send word to my Uncle Larkin Lealand in Death Valley when you arrive in Oregon, he'll be sure to get it to me."

"Promise me then, Alda, promise me this isn't goodbye, and you will come and visit us in Oregon."

"All right, I promise."

"Did you hear that, girls? Miss Alda promises she will come and visit when we get to our new home."

Ruby and Pearl scampered from the back of the wagon and over the sides.

Alda folded them into her arms and kissed the top of each one of their heads. "I'm going to miss you girls."

"I'm going to miss you, too," Pearl said and nuzzled her face into Alda's waist.

"Me, too," said Ruby.

Alda snugged the girls against her hips once more before their mother lifted each one back into the wagon and climbed up onto the seat.

Alda watched and waved as each wagon passed, the creak of their wheels the only sound above the tromp of the animals' hooves as they rounded the bend and drove out of sight. Turning back to her camp, Alda folded the bills Silas had handed her on his way by and put them in her front pocket. The twenty-five dollars wouldn't last long if she wasn't careful.

Midmorning, Alda tugged Bessie to a stop in front of the Cheyenne County Hospital. She tied the reins to the front rail and marched down the boardwalk to the second building. "You can stare all you want," she said under her breath as the men stopped shovelling to watch her progress. She planned to march upstairs, family or no family, and find out how Cord was faring.

With a swift shove, Alda opened the main doors and continued into the foyer and up to the desk where she stopped and put her hands on her hips.

The same young nurse sat at the desk. She paused, her pen in the air, and tipped her head to study Alda. The corners of her mouth curved up as she returned to her writing and spoke. "She's busy in Ward Two. You have about twenty minutes."

Alda sprinted up the stairs and rushed through the door of Ward Four. Six pairs of eyes scrutinized her arrival.

"Alda?" Cord was sitting next to his bed on a padded chair. "You got somebody chasing you?"

She cleared her throat and straightened her back before smoothing the front of her skirt. "I didn't realize you had roommates." There would be no stopping the pink procession from her neck up to her scalp. "Sorry," she said as she smiled at the five other patients in the room.

"You've been here before? Come have a seat." He patted the smooth top of his hospital bed.

Alda sat down. Her stomach quivered at Cord's nearness. He looked much better than he had on her first visit. His cheeks had filled out and returned to their natural tan color.

"Is that your sister, Cord?" a man called out from a bed behind the potbellied stove. A thick white bandage wrapped around his head and over one eye. Blood stained the bandage in uneven patches. "The head nurse says only family in this ward; you didn't mention being married."

"Horace, you old boot. Leave the man alone. You're just sore because your kin are as ugly as you are," said the patient in the third bed down from Cord. Both of his arms were wrapped in plaster casts to his fingertips. He shot Alda a gap-toothed grin before throwing another insult at Horace.

The room erupted as the men bantered back and forth on the attributes of each other's families.

Cord lifted his shoulders and let them drop. "You'll have to excuse us. We get mighty bored sitting here day after day. When did you come by before?"

Of course, the nurse hadn't mentioned her visit. It probably would've broken another rule. "Joshua brought me to the hospital the morning after you were hurt. You look much better today. How are you feeling?"

"Other than immense pain when I try and move this leg?" he rested a hand on the blanket draped over his lap.

Cord's naked ankles and feet peeked out from under the blanket. Alda quickly turned her gaze back to his face.

"I feel fine. The doctor says I should be able to leave tomorrow. Well," his Adam's apple bobbed, "that's if the doctor's confident he can leave me in capable hands." Cord's gaze sought Alda's, and then he reached out to wrap one large hand around both of hers.

Alda's breaths quickened. Should she tell Cord about her newfound faith in the Lord? Or should she tell him about the desire to become his wife? Maybe he would think she was trying to take advantage of his weakened state. Maybe his comments about a life together were simply the musings of a single man. She opened her mouth to speak.

The door burst open, and the pernicious nurse from Alda's first visit hustled into the room.

Alda drew her hands back from Cord's — so much for twenty minutes.

"You're in for it now, Cord," Horace said. "The prison warden is back."

The nurse pointed her finger at Alda. "You again! I thought I told you this ward was family only," she said, a finger poke in the air accenting each word. "We have rules to protect our patients. All these men are at grave risk of infection." She pointed toward the door. "Leave immediately!"

"Miss Harfield, Miss Lealand's only here to make arrangements to pick me up tomorrow. My wagon train's pulling out."

"They left today — "

"I don't care why she's here." She stomped over to the door and opened it. "Miss Lealand, you must leave."

Alda rose from the bed.

Cord wrinkled his brow. "They left? Without us?"

Alda walked backward toward the door, answering in a rush. "They couldn't stay any longer; they didn't know when you would be able to travel again."

The nurse grabbed Alda's upper arm.

Cord tossed a thick billfold toward Alda. It landed at her feet. Wrenching her arm from the nurse's hold, Alda scooped it from the ground.

The nurse regained her hold on Alda's arm and forced her through the open door.

"Buy a wagon, and come back tomorrow morning," Cord said as the door closed in Alda's face.

Chapter Thirteen

A few blocks from the hospital, Alda dismounted from Bessie's saddle in front of Abney's Livery Stable. The white, clapboard building with three sets of elk antlers adorning the false front was recommended by one of the hospital grounds workers.

Cord's thick wallet was heavy in her drawstring handbag. She'd traced the beautifully scrolled PCS tooled across the front several times before tucking it in her bag. Most likely the C was for Cord; apparently it wasn't even his first name. The man continued to remain a mystery to her.

Buy a wagon, he'd said. And then what? Boss could pull it over the narrow mountainous pass with Alda driving and a wounded man in the back? He must have more faith in her abilities than she did.

A rangy young man walked out of the double doors labeled Office. "What can I do for you, Ma'am?"

Alda handed over Bessie's reins. "Could you give my mule some grain and a good brushing?"

"I can do that," he said and slapped Bessie's hind end.

Bessie twitched her ears and looked at Alda. Her eyes were big brown pools begging her not to leave her in the care of such an imbecile.

Sorry, Bessie, I have business to attend to. "Could you take Bessie over to the blacksmith? She is in desperate need of new shoes."

"I can do that, too. I'll need you to pay up front for the smithing, though. It'll cost you a dollar fifty."

Alda pried the top of her drawstring bag and pulled out Cord's wallet. Upon unfolding it, a thick wad of bills was revealed.

The young man whistled. "That's a load of cash you got there."

Alda quickly withdrew one of the five dollar bills tucked in front of the many hundred and five hundred dollar denominations and closed the wallet. She handed the bill to the young man and added a stern note to her voice. "I'll expect the difference in sacks of grain."

"Yes, Ma'am," he said before leading Bessie toward the open barn doors several feet down from the office doors.

Alda returned Cord's wallet to her bag. Even that quick glimpse had told her the wallet held thousands of dollars. Had the man never heard of a bank? There was enough money to ship Alda and the mules home, pay the taxes on the farm, and live comfortably for years. Her father would have said fortune had smiled brightly on her this fine morning.

Cord wouldn't come for the money either. She knew that as sure as she knew anything. It would break his heart if she stole it, but she would just be one more person he needed to forgive.

Alda strode across the dusty avenue toward Sixteenth Street where she'd been told she could find most anything. *Not today, Pa.* She wouldn't betray the man she claimed to love nor would she disappoint the God Who declared to love her.

The business district of Cheyenne trailed along the top of a hill overlooking a shallow valley. The buildings along Sixteenth Street ranged from narrow, one-window wooden shops to two-story brick hotels.

Alda stepped onto the busy boardwalk and passed several shop fronts before slipping into a ladies wear store to purchase three pairs of drawers. She'd reduced all her own pairs and several of her mother's to tatters. How was she to know sitting in the saddle, day after day, was not kind to underclothes? She would restore the funds she spent on herself from her own meager funds when she returned to camp.

As Alda left the ladies wear store with a brown paper parcel under her arm, her eye caught the backside of a man turning the corner. His gait looked familiar. Walker? Alda rushed to the corner and peered around it. The man wasn't in the alley. It couldn't be Walker; his father sent him home a week ago.

She shook her head and continued down to the mercantile to buy a new handkerchief for Cord. Ruby had refused to return the one he had wrapped around her hand for a bandage.

She already missed the girls. The wagon train would be well into the pass by now. Maybe, if she and Cord left first thing in the morning, they would be able to catch up with the others in a day or two. Why was she lying to herself? Cord wouldn't be able to travel far, if he could travel at all.

An hour later, as Alda left the bakery, she lifted a warm loaf of bread to her nose, closed her eyes, and sniffed it through the wrapper. "Mmmmm." It smelled just like Mamma's fresh baked bread. Alda hadn't eaten yeast-raised bread since she'd left home. It would make a wonderful treat with her supper.

"Pardon me," she said to the chest she walked in to.

"I'm not sure I will."

Alda leapt back, and her packages fell to the ground. "Walker? What are you doing here?"

Walker pushed his shoulders back and grasped the edges of his cutaway jacket. A gold watch chain curved from his striped vest pocket to his matching striped pants pocket. He wore a black bowler hat and bow tie.

With quaking hands, Alda bent to the sidewalk and

gathered her packages. If only Cord were with her. She stood and faced Walker. "I thought you went home."

"My pa thought I did, too." His eyes raked over her body. "But I had unfinished business to attend to."

"I'll let you be about it then," Alda said, clutching her parcels tightly as she attempted to pass by.

He stepped in front of her.

"Walker, let me pass," she whispered.

"Surely you don't want to cause a scene," he snarled back.

Alda looked at the passers-by; several were throwing them curious glances.

Without warning, Walker's arm encircled her shoulders. "Sweetheart," he said, "let me take your burdens for you." He deftly plucked the packages from her and drew her a couple of steps down the sidewalk to a waiting carriage. He picked her up, opened the door, and carried her in.

With a snap of the reins, the carriage took off down the graveled street. Alda pushed her bonnet back from her eyes and rose from her hands and knees on the floor where she'd been plunked. The closed curtains swayed as the carriage bounced and jolted. Alda collected her parcels from the floor and placed them on the bench before grabbing the leather loop hanging from the ceiling to right herself.

Walker slipped the upper latch on the door.

"Stop this carriage and let me out!"

"Please, Alda dear, I mean you no harm. Take a seat." He patted the space next to him.

Alda plopped down on the opposite bench.

"Still feisty, I see."

The smarm in his voice caused her lunch to snake its way up her throat. "What do want?" she asked.

"Like I said before, I want us to spend time together — a lot of time together. In fact, I've arranged for a small ceremony in a lovely garden on the outskirts of town."

Was he insane? "Ceremony?" Her voice ascended to a higher pitch. "As in marriage ceremony?"

He tweaked his bow tie and swallowed. "It's along the creek. Mrs. Hewit has promised to serve lemonade and tea cakes afterwards."

Alda brought both her hands to her to chest. Her breathing accelerated. "No!"

A look of surprise crossed Walker's features. He threw his arms out in a wide arc. "What do you mean, no?"

"No. I won't marry you — ever."

"Why not?"

Because you are not Cord. "I don't love you."

"I'm sure over time — "

"No, not even over time, Walker. Be reasonable and tell the driver to stop the carriage and let me go."

Ice filled his bright blue eyes. "It's Cord, isn't it? Cord is the reason you won't marry me."

She couldn't tell him the truth. "No, I won't marry you because I don't love you." His cold stare terrified her. What was he thinking? *Lord, please keep me safe.*

"Humph," he said and pushed his upper lip into a mocking sneer. "Are you certain you won't change your mind?"

"Yes. I'm certain."

"Then, my sweet, you leave me no other choice."

Walker twisted the latch on the window and flung his arm out. The coach slowed.

"Are you going to let me go?"

"No, the driver's merely heading to the second location I gave, earlier in my instructions." Walker smirked a second time. "He looked quite surprised by the options."

The carriage turned around, throwing Alda's head against the sidewall and her parcels to the floor. "Ouch," she said and rubbed the spot where the wall had connected and then picked her parcels up from the floor once more. "What options?"

"Beautiful garden or county jail."

"County jail? It's not a crime not to marry you."

"So you haven't seen the posters?"

Posters? Why would there be wanted posters with her picture on them?

"Understandable," Walker said. "I took them down as I found them. I didn't want people looking at my new *wife* as a criminal. Although, it wasn't a great likeness; it didn't show the color of your pretty hair." He leaned forward and touched the stray lock cascading down her cheek.

Alda jerked her head away and then pressed her fingers to her temples. "I'm getting a headache. Would you please tell me what you're talking about?"

Walker pulled a folded paper from his pants pocket and handed it to Alda. As she unfolded it, the bold words struck her like a blow.

Reward \$100 for the Capture of Alda Lealand
Horse Thief
Wanted for the theft of prize winning mules
A handsome, petite woman, about 5 ft. 3 inches tall
with flaming red hair
Contact the Wayne City, Missouri Sheriff

Her pa? Alda's stomach rolled. Why did he do it? He was the one who had abandoned her, left her with hardly a penny. The county was going to take their home. Didn't he care? The poster shook in her fingers.

Walker snatched it from her hand and refolded it as he spoke, "A pittance really, the one hundred dollar reward; hardly worth my trouble." Walker picked a piece of lint from his lapel. "My father doesn't spare any expense when it comes to his only son. You could've had a part in his generosity."

There wasn't enough money in the world to convince her to marry Walker.

His eyes narrowed as though he could read her thoughts. "I think there will be a certain amount of satisfaction in turning you in."

The carriage slowed to a stop, and Walker pushed the curtain aside to peer out. "We've arrived, Alda." He lifted the latch and opened the door. "After you," he said.

Alda swept her skirt up in a bunch, descended onto the step, and launched herself from the carriage. When her boots hit the gravel, she ran.

"Hey!" Walker yelled.

Alda could hear his boots grind the gravel as he chased her down the road.

"I ought to whoop you when I catch you."

A few steps later his hand wound around her arm and wrenched her to a stop. Alda's chest heaved as she bent to catch her breath. "Walker, let me go." She sucked in another breath. "I'll give you the hundred dollars, and I won't hold this incident against you," she said and stood to face Walker whose face had turned the color of beets. "I won't hold hurting Cord against you either."

He wrenched her arm again as he tugged her toward the sheriff's office door. "No deal. I can live with the guilt."

Alda dug her heels in and strained at the pull of his hand. Walker tightened his grip.

"You need any help, Sir?" the coach driver asked. "She's a handful."

Walker yanked her arm, and a spike of pain shot through her shoulder.

"She'll behave, if she knows what's good for her."

Alda laughed.

Walker tugged her arm harder, and her feet stumbled over one another. "You can come back in about half an hour," he said to the driver.

Alda stared at the approaching door. What would happen to the mules if she was taken into custody? Cord was waiting on her, too. Hard to believe her pa would turn her in. Ma was probably turning over in her grave right now. Her pa was a lot of things, but she never took him for a traitor.

Walker tugged the heavy metal door open and hauled her through the doorway. A narrow faced deputy with a droopy mustache sat with his feet up on a desk reading a newspaper.

He swung his feet to the ground and put the paper on the desk. As his eyes swept up her body in an appraisal, he pushed out his lower lip and nodded.

Alda lowered her eyes at his forthright assessment.

"What did she do to ya?" he asked.

Walker pulled the folded poster from his pocket and snapped it out while keeping a tight grip on Alda's arm. He handed the poster to the deputy.

As the deputy read the words, his eyebrows shot up and he leaned back to take Alda in again. "You sure this is her? Doesn't look much like her." He laid the poster on the desk.

Walker pushed Alda toward the desk. "It's her. Where do I get my hundred bucks?"

"Is this you?" the deputy poked at the poster.

Alda kept her head down. He could ask all he wanted; she didn't have to answer.

The deputy adjusted the bulky wad of snuff in his lower lip before speaking. "Looks like the woman's not quite sure who she is," he said to Walker.

"She's sure all right. She just doesn't want to say." Walker tugged the back of Alda's bonnet snapping her head up. "Tell the deputy you're the pathetic thief who stole from her own family."

Alda bit the inside of her lip to keep from speaking her mind.

Walker jabbed the center of her back, and she staggered forward. "Tell him!" he boomed.

"Settle down, Sir. We don't hold with abusing women

here — any kind of woman."

Alda turned to make sure Walker saw the smile on her face.

"You give us your full name and whereabouts, and the sheriff will see to it you get your reward," the deputy said to Walker. He shuffled through a stack of papers on the corner of the desk, picked one out, and handed it over. "Fill in this form and leave it with me."

Walker looked like he wanted to snuff the life out of her as he reached for the paper.

Why did he need the money so bad if his pa *spared no expense,* like he said? Maybe he'd spent too much money on fancy clothes, or maybe it was a lie like most of the words coming out of Walker's mouth. "Deputy, I'd like to report an attempted murder."

The deputy's eyes bulged in their sockets. "An attempted murder?"

"This man caused the goring and near death of a man of the law." *Sorry, Cord.* The statement held more weight if she revealed his secret.

Walker jeered, "A man of the law, hey?"

"Are you a witness, Ma'am?"

"Deputy are you going to take the word of a horse thief," he pointed to the poster on the desk.

Alda's palm shot out, and she slapped Walker across the cheek. "I'm no horse thief!"

"Deputy, you saw that," Walker squeezed his hand into a fist. "I'm of a mind to teach this woman a lesson."

The deputy stepped between Alda and Walker. "Like I said, we don't abuse women here."

"But you saw what she did to me." A red welt was forming on Walker's cheek.

"And you did what you came for. Now take the paperwork, fill it out, and bring it back later."

Walker scowled at Alda over the deputy's shoulder before turning away and stomping out the door.

The deputy pulled a worn, rush seated chair from the wall and indicated for her to sit down. Alda removed her bonnet and folded it on her lap. The deputy ogled her curls briefly before sitting behind the desk.

"About the attempted murder," he spit in the brass spittoon against the wall. "Did you see it?"

"No, but I know he did it."

"Anybody else see it?"

Walker wasn't a fool. He would've waited until he and Cord were alone. It would be Cord's word against Walker's. "Only the man he did it to, and he's a little worse for wear. You'll find him at the county hospital; his name is Cord, and he's a bounty hunter."

"Bounty hunter? You left that out of the story, didn't you?"

"He's still a recognized part of law enforcement, isn't he?

"Not everyone thinks so, but I hear ya."

"I'm supposed to pick him up in the morning. We are on our way to Death Valley to sell the mules."

The deputy rocked back in his chair. "The mules you stole. So I take it you would be …" he dropped the chair legs to the floor, picked up the poster from the desk, and perused it, "Miss Alda Lealand, like our good friend said." He winked.

Drat, it wasn't like she could keep the deputy in the dark much longer anyway. "Sir, do I look like a thief to you?" Alda resisted the urge to squirm under the frank appraisal of the deputy.

Ting, a wad of tobacco juice hit the spittoon. "Not particularly."

"If you let me go, I'll be on my way, and I won't cause you any trouble." Alda stood, wound the cord from her purse around her hand and stepped to the side preparing to leave.

"Ma'am, you know I can't do that. Woman or no

woman, the law doesn't look kindly on horse thieves. You can be thankful whoever reported the theft only wanted your capture and not to have you swing at the end of a rope."

The deputy pointed at the chair, and Alda took a seat, again. "You'll have to excuse me, Sir, if I'm not grateful. It was my own father who went to the law."

The deputy lifted his Stetson and rubbed his forehead. "Your own pa?"

"My ma died about a month ago, and the county is threatening a tax sale of our farm. My pa took off to Excelsior Springs without a thought about me or the property. Selling the mules was my uncle's idea, and I convinced my ma I could handle the drive to California. It's her brother who's brokered the deal in Death Valley. I'm telling you, Sir, it's all on the up and up." Alda lifted a couple inches off of the chair.

"Doesn't matter."

Alda dropped back to her seat.

"It's a sad story, if it's the truth," he raised an eyebrow and nodded, "but the wheels of justice have started in motion. I'm going to have to put you under arrest, and you'll have to spend some time in our…" he tapped the side of his nose with his forefinger, "… fine establishment until the sheriff figures out what to do with you."

Alda covered her mouth with her hand. Her own pa was sending her to a jail cell? The room spun.

"… he can decide then if he's going to send you to court here in Cheyenne or send you back home to face the bench."

Alda shook her head to hold back the nausea. "Pardon, when will he decide?"

"The sheriff's not back for a couple of days. So I guess you know where you're sleeping tonight. I'll have to take your personal belongings. Do you have any weapons on you?"

Alda dropped her gaze to her hands.

"I can bring a woman in to search you if need be."

"No, I don't have any weapons. I've got a shot gun with my things back at the camp. I wish I had brought it in with me today. If I had, Walker would've gotten what's coming to him."

"You're fiery, I'll give you that, but you and I know you don't mean a word of what you just said."

The deputy was right. It wasn't her place to send Walker to meet his judgment. She'd never been able to kill the chickens for supper, let alone a grown man.

"Put your things on the desk. We'll keep good care of them." The deputy opened a drawer and pulled out a muslin bag.

Alda put her bonnet on the desk and then her drawstring bag. She unclasped her mother's gold locket from her neck and laid it on the desk alongside her bonnet.

The deputy recorded her bonnet and necklace on a piece of paper and reached for her purse.

Please put the purse in the bag.

The deputy picked up her purse and then shook it. "Carrying a bit of a load, aren't you? I thought you said you didn't have any weapons on you."

Alda stared at her purse, willing the Deputy to put it in the muslin bag.

The deputy put her purse on the desk and stuffed his large fingers into the top ruffle. After prying the purse open, he pulled out Cord's thick wallet.

Alda shut her eyes and winced — waiting for what was coming.

The deputy opened Cord's wallet and set it on the desk. "Stand up."

She stood and the deputy yanked her hands together behind her back. Alda twisted her neck over her shoulder to speak. "I can explain; it's not mine."

"I'm quite certain it's not. The question is where's the

fool you took it from?"

"It's the bounty hunter's. The one I told you who's in the hospital."

"Is there a good reason you happen to be carrying his fortune about?"

Alda opened her mouth to retort. What could she say? They were friends? She wanted to marry him? "Uuuuhh, I was supposed to buy a wagon."

The deputy reached over and fanned through the money in the wallet, most likely doing a quick calculation.

"Did you say one wagon or a hundred wagons? Time to go." He grabbed her left elbow and dragged her toward a door in the middle of the adjacent wall.

The door revealed a wide hallway with six jail cells along one side. Each jail cell door consisted of thick metal bars forming a grid of rectangles, which were painted white as though they would make a stay behind one more palatable. An eight-inch slot stood about head height in every door.

A man wreaking of alcohol and wearing stained clothing clung to the bars of the first cell. "Well, I'll be. We don't see many of your kind in this place. Deputy, you can put this fine woman in my cell if you like. I don't mind sharing." His leer revealed a mouthful of rotted teeth as he reached through the bars with his dirty fingers.

Alda pulled at the deputy's hold to distance herself from the man's reach.

The deputy jerked her back in front of him, and they proceeded down the hallway. "Lewis, behave yourself," he said. After pulling a ring of keys from his belt, he opened the fourth cell door.

Alda's spirits fell as she took in the small cell containing only a rough wooden bench with a thin blanket and a tin ware chamber pot. The deputy released her wrists and pushed her into the cell. She turned back and grabbed his sleeve, "Sir, could you please make sure my mules are cared for?"

The deputy shook from her grasp and let the jail cell door clang into place as Alda continued to plead.

"They're out by the lake. If you send them to Abney's, I'll see to it they get paid when my pa clears all this up."

The key scraped in the lock, and the deputy headed back down the hallway.

Alda gripped the cold bars with both hands. "Sir, please, my mules; and there's a grey gelding out there, too. It belongs to the man I told you about. The horse's name is Boss."

"Any chance I could get a glass of something stronger than water," Lewis asked as the deputy passed his cell.

The deputy exited the hall without a word.

Alda lay down on the bench and pulled the blanket up to her chin. *Lord, please take care of Bessie, Moses, Old Joe, Arthur, Jenny, Bud, Gideon, Jeremiah, and Boss, too.*

Chapter Fourteen

Cord leaned back against the shiplap of the tailor shop and caught his breath. The blood pounding through his upper thigh made the injury hurt like blazes. It had taken him over an hour and a half to stumble his way from the hospital to Main Street. It was a good thing Horace had agreed to distract Miss Harfield for at least half an hour with the screams of a man on his death bed. He'd practiced thrashing from side to side and gasping for air earlier that morning for the rest of the patients. The men agreed it looked believable enough.

Alda hadn't shown up yesterday, or today. Cord couldn't pay his bill, not having a cent on him, and he couldn't stay one more minute under Miss Harfield's thumb. He'd snuck out the back stairway, albeit slowly, a couple of minutes before Horace's performance began.

Where had Alda gone? There was no way she would have taken his money and left town … although seven thousand dollars could be quite a temptation. He should have put the money in the bank with the rest of his savings when he'd had the chance. What if—

"Sir, are you all right?" a young woman holding the hand of a small boy stopped to ask.

"I'm fine, Ma'am."

"You appear to be bleeding." The woman pointed to Cord's leg. Blood had seeped through his waist overalls and made a large crimson patch.

"I guess I'll have to see to that. Thank you, Ma'am." He nodded, and the woman continued down the boardwalk. Cord clenched his jaw and straightened his back to take a few more steps to the hotel next door. Fancy black letters above the second-story windows spelled Rollins House. He opened the door and approached the counter slowly. As he leaned on the burled walnut counter to take the weight off his injured leg, a freckled young man looked up from the columns of numbers he was studying in a large black book.

"May I help you?"

"I need a room for the night, on the first floor."

The young man placed a register on the counter. "Sign here," he said.

As Cord scribbled Wilson Newey below the last customer, the young man turned around in his chair and plucked a key from the key board. "You can have room four, down that hallway." He indicated with a bob of his head toward a wide, plush hallway extending from an archway across from the desk.

It looked two miles long. "Could you have someone pick up several rolls of bandages and a new pair of denim waist overalls and bring them to my room?"

The young man narrowed his eyes as though contemplating the request. "I suppose so."

Cord pulled a dollar coin from his pocket and handed it to the clerk. "Thank you," he said. A sweat broke out on his brow and rivulets of blood trickled down his leg by the time he hobbled to his room and laid down on the bed. *Alda, where are you?* he asked as his eyelids fell.

~

Cord's brow furrowed as he took in Alda's listing tent and her packs stacked neatly to the side. After hiring a hansom and driving to the bank to dip into his savings, Cord had asked the driver to take him out to the lake. The mules were gone, and so was Boss. Alda wouldn't have left her supplies behind. Or maybe she would, if she'd hightailed it out of town with his wallet. He was starting to think maybe the temptation had been too much for her. The money, he could almost handle, taking his horse … He kicked at a lump of dirt and nearly lost his balance as a surge of pain roared up his right leg. The morning's pain killers had worn off — completely. He'd have to look into more if he was going to get anywhere.

Cord and the driver loaded his pack, bedroll, and saddle bags into the hansom before Cord struggled back into the cab. He asked the driver to halt beside the only inhabited campsite comprised of two covered wagons. A man and two women sat around the fire while a handful of children ran around and in between the wagons. "Any chance you folks seen the person camping over yonder in that tent?"

The man took the chop he was gnawing on from his mouth and wiped the grease from his chin with the back of his hand. "Nope. We've been here two days. Got some sick young'uns in the wagons; we're waiting until they're better before we move on. We haven't seen a single soul over there."

Both women shook their heads without speaking.

Cord pulled a ten dollar bill from his pocket and held it out. "Would you send word to the Rollins Hotel, care of room four, if somebody shows? I'm looking for a friend of mine." At least he thought she was a friend — much more than a friend. How could he have been such a fool?

"You don't need to pay me for that, Sir."

Cord waved the bill. "I know, maybe you can call a doctor to come and check on your children. You'll be doing me a favor."

Relief washed over the man's face as he took the ten dollar bill from Cord's hand. "Thank you, Sir." The man removed his battered felt hat and held it over his chest. "You don't know how much this means to us. The Lord go with you."

Cord nodded and indicated for the driver to move on.

With a snap of the reins, they headed back toward town.

He needed something to eat that didn't involve beef broth. If Nurse Harfield had her way, the whole population would have to survive on the stuff. He never wanted to see another bowl of it as long as he lived. His stomach grumbled as though in agreement.

After buying the driver lunch, Cord asked him to stop by the hospital. He sent the driver in to pay his bill and get a prescription for some pain pills. There was no way Cord was going through those doors again in case the doc, or Nurse Harfield, thought he needed more medical attention.

The bag of candies he'd sent for the men in Ward Four would have to do as a thank you to Horace and the others for their cooperation in helping him escape. He'd miss the entertainment they'd provided in the last week and a half.

After stopping at the apothecary, Cord asked the driver to drop him off at the hotel so he could take a pain pill, soak in a good hot bath, and then figure out what to do about Alda.

A bell boy unloaded Cord's belongings from the cab and carried them to his room. Cord followed, holding his breath and tensing his muscles as he crossed the hotel lobby. The sooner the pain pills worked — the better.

"Sir," the young clerk called out. "A young man stopped by and left a message for you."

"A young man?"

"A scrap of boy with his sleeves up to here." The clerk tapped well above his wrists. "He said you'd done the family a favor."

The family by the lake. "What did he say?"

The clerk placed a worn and folded scrap of paper on the counter. Cord picked up the note and read the scrawled message.

> Sir,
>
> Our neighboring camp returned. They haven't seen

anybody either, but some deputies came by two days ago and loaded up a pack of mules and a grey gelding they thought belonged to the same camp you were wondering about.
Sincerely,
Oliver Younger, A thankful father.

Deputies? Why would the sheriff's department be moving the animals? Maybe Alda hadn't taken off with his money after all. Maybe something had happened to her. Cord's chest tightened at the thought of Alda being hurt, or worse. That girl had a knack for getting into tight spots.

"Where's the sheriff's office?"

The clerk wasn't surprised by the question; so much for hotel patron's privacy.

"It's three blocks over on Nineteenth Street. Any driver in this city will know where it is."

Ten minutes later, Cord descended from another cab and walked slowly toward the black metal door of the sheriff's office.

A slim deputy with a walrus mustache narrowed one eye as Cord limped toward his desk. "May I help you, Sir?" he asked.

Cord swallowed as the pit of his innards sunk to his toes. A long, dark red curl lay on the corner of the deputies' desk. *No, Lord, please let it not be Alda's.* Cord swallowed again, and his fingers shook slightly as reached out to pluck the curl from the desk. "Where's the woman who belongs to this?" *Alda, I'm sorry for doubting you. I should've known you were made of better stuff than your pa.*

The deputy's cheeks colored as he snatched the curl from Cord's fingers. "She's not here. I took this for evidence."

Cord took the curl back from the deputy and tucked it into his vest pocket. As he leaned forward to put his fists on the desk, he growled, "Evidence of what?"

"Look, I don't have to answer *your* questions."

Cord mustered up an intimidating stare. He didn't have the strength to follow through on it, but maybe the deputy wouldn't figure that out. "Where is she?"

"What's it to you? She's a common horse thief — thief in general. We're trying to sort out the details. In the meantime, the sheriff sent her to the territorial prison in Laramie."

Alda's alive! "Has she been convicted?"

"Not yet, but she will be shortly. We couldn't keep her here. She was causing too much of a ruckus with the other inmates. They've got other women prisoners over in Laramie."

"Who's calling her a horse thief?"

The deputy pointed to a poster amongst the others tacked to the wall beside the desk. The word *caught* was scrawled across Alda's picture.

He read the words as Alda's accusing eyes stared back at him. "This have anything to do with a fellow named Walker?" If it did, Walker better hope he had some deep, dark cave to climb into, and he better never climb out either.

"Nope, but he's the fellow who turned her in."

So he didn't leave for home like his pa said. Not surprising. Walker's mean streak wouldn't have let Cord and Alda alone without some sort of retribution. "So who went to the law?"

"According to the sheriff in Wayne City, and the girl herself, it was her pa."

"Her pa?"

"They were his mules."

That sorry, son of a — "He turned on his own daughter?"

"It's probably his opinion that she turned first. But it nearly broke her heart, I can tell you that. The girl prayed night and day in that cell."

"Prayed?" The word caught in his throat. *Lord, thank You for being there with Alda. Thank You for drawing that sweet girl to Yourself. Please, let me help her.* "Did the sheriff contact her pa? See if he could straighten out the misunderstanding?"

"Yeah, he did. It seems there's no misunderstanding." The deputy slid a Western Union telegram across the desk.

Sheriff Charles Dunn,
Cheyenne, Wyoming Territory

It is my intent to have Alda Lealand, horse thief, prosecuted to the full extent of the law.

Ira Lealand
Wayne City, Missouri

Cord reread the words and shook his head. What would possess her pa to do it?

"The sheriff doesn't want to put her in front of the bench until he figures out what to do about the money. Walker brought her in with a wallet full. She gave us a story about a bounty hunter." He paused and eyed Cord before continuing. "I went to the hospital the day before yesterday, but it seems the man checked himself out." The deputy spit a wad of tobacco juice into a brass spittoon. "The fellow had a leg injury."

"It's my wallet. I gave it to Alda to buy a wagon to take over the pass. I can't ride yet."

"It's a lot of money to hand over. She your sweetheart?"

Interesting question considering the man had a locket of Alda's hair on the corner of his desk. "I plan to marry that girl," Cord said.

"Marry?" The deputy's voice went up a notch. "That'll take some doing seeing as she's in prison."

"I'll go find her pa, help him change his mind." Buy him out, return the mules, whatever it took to make Alda his own. "The wallet was no crime."

"So you say. Any chance you could tell me the initials on the wallet and how much money was in it."

"Black leather billfold bearing the initials P. C. S. I had about seven thousand dollars in it. Money earned from bounty hunting — like she said."

"Sounds about right. I'm not sure why I'm satisfied with being a deputy, it looks like the bounty hunting business is a lot more lucrative."

"Sure, if you don't mind being on the trail day and night and not having people who count on you."

The deputy sucked some tobacco juice through his stained front teeth. "I thought you said you were getting married. How's that going to work for you?"

Good question. Cord returned the direct stare of the deputy. "You'll have to leave that to me to figure out, now won't you? How long do I have before she's in front of a judge?"

The deputy shrugged. "I suppose she's not going anywhere. I can stall the sheriff for … maybe a week," a wide grin spread across his face, "for the sake of true love."

Cord gave a quick nod. "I appreciate it."

"Good luck convincing her father to withdraw the accusation. If you do, bring a legal document to show the sheriff."

"Can I have my wallet?"

"You can ask the sheriff about that when you return."

Cord shuffled to his waiting cab and directed the driver to return to the Rollins. After paying his bill and clearing his room, they drove to the train station; last stop, a pretty little farm, with fields full of mules, a couple of miles south of the river — Wayne City, Missouri.

Chapter Fifteen

When the hand bell rang, Alda rolled over and groaned. The icy cold of the hewn stone jail cell crawled through every muscle in her body at night. It didn't help that the thin mattress of her prison bunk didn't even begin to disguise the ropes underneath. She flexed her fingers and then rubbed her arms to warm them.

"You all right, little one? I'd like to say the nights will get easier, but I'd be lying if I did." Her roommate Rosie sat up and pulled her fingers through to the ends of her long hair.

Rosie's hair was the color of coffee and cream — what Alda wouldn't give for one of Cord's coffees right now. She could wrap her hands around the warmth of the cup and enjoy his smile from across its rim. Where was he and was he thinking of her? By now he'd probably decided she wasn't worth the trouble, and he was probably right.

Alda would have liked to run her fingers through her own hair — if she had any. Flea infestation aside, she might have gone too far with the self-recriminations. The deputy back in Cheyenne looked like he wanted to cry when she handed him her chamber pot full of red curls. He should've known a knife was easy enough to come by in a jail full of lawbreakers. What had possessed her to cut her hair all off down to the scalp though? She still wasn't certain, but her pa's betrayal had sliced her through to the core.

"Are you going to pray this morning?" Rosie asked.

Alda lifted the wool blanket and slid to the cold floor to kneel beside Rosie. "Lord, I thank You for a new day. I thank You for filling our hearts with the comfort of Your Spirit. Lord, be with Rosie's children."

Rosie's chest heaved with a sob, and Alda put her arm around the woman's thin shoulders.

"Lord, we know You can keep them safe and fed. Help me to forgive my pa like You have forgiven me. Amen."

Rosie mumbled amen and began the morning's routine.

If only Alda could spend a few more minutes in bed, lumps and all, but the women's guard, Mrs. Snellen, would be doing inspections in fifteen minutes. The beds needed to be tidied and both women dressed before they were allowed their turn at the toilets.

Alda spent a few of the fifteen minutes every morning staring out the barred window toward the snow-capped Rockies — her thoughts in silent praise for the Keeper of her soul. Pastor Heaton's favorite verse played through her mind. "I will lift up mine eyes unto the hills, from whence cometh my help. My help cometh from the Lord, which made heaven and earth."

"Do you think today's the day?" Rosie asked.

"Rosie, I want to help you and your children, you know I do. But I don't know if Cord will ever come and find me. I could be giving you false hope. He's a generous man, I told you the truth about that, but I've got nothing left to offer him, and he might have figured that out by now."

It was Rosie's turn to put her arms around Alda. "You know that's not true." Rosie squeezed Alda's shoulders. "I agree, waking up in this place is enough to make any situation look hopeless, but what did you read to me the other day, something about not to be afraid because the Lord would help us."

"The verse in Isaiah, 'Fear thou not: for I am with thee: be not dismayed; for I am thy God: I will strengthen thee;

yea, I will help thee.'" Alda had memorized the verse the same morning they'd read it from the Bible, a Bible gifted to Alda and Rosie by a group of settlers on their way to Oregon. The womenfolk had toured the prison to pass the time waiting for wagon repairs in Laramie.

Although grateful for the scriptures, being peered at through the bars like some sort of dangerous circus animal bothered both Rosie and Alda.

"You're right, I should believe what we've read, or there's no point in reading it." Since they'd been given the gift, Rosie and Alda had spent many of their waking hours poring over the Word. Other than three meals a day, with the other women prisoners, they were kept locked up twenty-four hours a day — for their own protection. It was enough to make Alda insane.

"There's no reason the Lord won't use Cord to give us some help, if he's as fine a man as you say he is."

"All right, Rosie, you win. Cord's going to come riding across the field on his horse Boss and rescue us both from the hands of Mrs. Snellen." Even though he can't ride. "In the meantime, we better get dressed or we'll miss out on the delightful gruel the cook likes to pass off as oatmeal."

~

Cord peered out the window of the coach as it slowed and turned onto a graveled drive. Alda was right; her home was a pretty little farm — well known, too. After only a couple of inquiries at the station, he'd found a driver who knew of Lealand Farms and where to find it along the Missouri River.

Dozens of mules grazed along a split rail fence in good repair. A tall, hip roofed barn with two adjacent paddocks held several draft horses munching hay. The drive continued to a modest two-story brick house. Several attractive flower gardens spread from the house onto the manicured lawns. Whether her pa was a scoundrel or not, he could see why Alda didn't want to lose the place.

The trip to Kansas City by train had taken only two days. Cord should have insisted on shipping Alda's mules to Death Valley by cars. Then again, he'd tried, and she wouldn't listen. Maybe now she would, if he could get her out of prison.

Cord asked the driver to wait. He probably assumed Cord was here to inquire into some of the *best Missouri mules south of the river*. Cord wasn't going to tell him any different.

Being off his feet had done his injury some good, although he hadn't gotten much sleep on the hard wooden benches of the passenger car. A corner of the curtain lifted in the front window as Cord limped down the flagstone walkway to the front door. He raised the ring on the mule's head door knocker to announce his arrival.

The door opened, pulling the ring out of his grasp, and an attractive, blond haired young woman giggled. "I see I've beaten you to it," she said.

Who was she? Alda said she was an only child.

The woman stepped through the door and offered her hand for a kiss. "I don't believe we've met, although my dearest has yet to introduce me to his friends."

Cord automatically took the woman's proffered hand, but he neglected to bend and kiss it until she tipped her head to the side and narrowed her eyes.

After doing so, he stepped back to introduce himself. "Forgive my manners; I wasn't expecting to see a woman in the home. I'm Preston Cordell Sweet the third."

"So, Preston Cordell Sweet the third," the woman batted long eyelashes not half as lovely as Alda's, "who were you expecting to see?"

"Melinda," a man's voice called out from inside the house, "who are you speaking with?"

"It's your friend, dear, Preston."

"Preston?" An older man with a stocky build and a full head of greyish black curls stepped into the hall, wiping his hands on a cotton rag. He walked toward Cord and the woman on the front walk with a look of puzzlement on his face. “I’m not sure we’ve met.” He paused the wiping of his hands.

Cord offered his right hand for a handshake, and the man ignored it. “I’m Cord Sweet, Sir, I was told this was Lealand Farm. I’m looking for Ira Lealand.”

“You’ve found him.”

“Ira Lealand, Alda Lealand’s father?”

“Melinda, go back in the house.”

“But, Ira, surely we can do the neighborly thing and invite the man in for tea.” Melinda
smiled demurely and reached up to tuck a stray lock of hair behind her ear.

“I said, go back in the house.”

Melinda picked up her skirts and flounced back through the doorway.

Alda’s father shut the door in Melinda’s wake. “What do you want? I don’t see any badge. Are you here for the sheriff’s department; have they found my mules?”

“What about your daughter, Sir? Are you concerned about her?”

“Alda made her choice; she knew better than to take off with my mules. You can’t fault me for doing the right thing and going to the law.”

“You don’t think it was a bit harsh? She thought she was doing the *right thing* and saving your farm.” Cord turned and swept his arm out to make the point.

Ira grunted. “Is that what she told you? She was saving the farm?”

“She told me you haven’t paid the taxes in three years, and the county is ready to foreclose.”

Ira’s neck began to color, and he raised his voice. “Now look here, that’s a family matter, and she has no business talking to anyone about family matters.” Ira took a stride toward Cord. “Who are you, and what do you have to do with my daughter?"

"Would getting married to a girl more than half your age before your wife's body is barely cold in the ground be a family matter? Perhaps something you should mention to your own kin? I can take the information back to Alda if you like. I can't say she'll be happy though. She seemed to think her ma sacrificed a lot for you."

Ira puffed out his chest and stepped within inches of Cord's face. "You better tell me what you're doing here, and tell me now."

The door opened, and Melinda popped her head out. "Ira, is everything all right out here."

"Get in the house," Ira snarled.

The door clicked shut.

Cord stayed put and met Ira's stony glare. "I'm here to save your daughter. She doesn't deserve to rot in some prison because you're too proud to admit she was trying to help."

Ira must've changed his mind about challenging Cord; he backed down and smirked. "Well, you can tell Alda my help just walked through that door." Ira motioned toward the front of the house. "Melinda came with a little nest egg. She wants to invest in making Lealand Farm Mules the best mules in the whole country."

The poor woman, she probably has no idea what she was in for. Maybe appealing to Ira's pride might work in Cord's favor. "I imagine you could use some help advertising then."

Ira's face perked up, and Cord could see the glimmer of interest in his eye. "What are you talking about?"

"Alda was taking the mules to Death Valley."

"Death Valley, California? What is that girl thinking?"

"They're hauling borax ore out of the valley with twenty mule teams. They need quality mules. People will be talking — they'll be talking about how your mules can handle the close to forty ton load better than any others.

And then they'll be clamoring for more."

Ira nodded his head as though in agreement. "But — "

"I expect you'd want payment for the mules and for your inconvenience." Cord pulled some cash out of his pocket and fanned the one hundred dollar bills.

Ira looked like he wanted to eat them up.

"Alda's Uncle Larkin has negotiated twelve hundred for the mules. I'll give you — "

"Larkin? My own brother's in on this?" Ira put his hands on his hips, the dirty rag rolled up in a ball in his fist. "I don't want your money; I want my mules."

Lord, give me patience. I'd much rather hit him than deal with him. "How does three thousand dollars sound to you?"

Ira's eyes widened. He appeared to be searching for words.

"All I need from you is a bill of sale for the mules and your signature on this letter to the sheriff in Cheyenne."

"So, you're telling me you're willing to pay more than four times the value of my mules."

"Yes, Sir, in cash."

"How much for my daughter?"

"Pardon?"

"It looks like you've got money and you're not buying my mules for my mule's sake, so how much for my daughter?"

What kind of a father asks a question like that? *Alda, forgive me*. Cord lowered his voice to a gruff whisper. "Another three thousand. That's three thousand for the mules and three thousand for your daughter Alda. I'll return tomorrow with six thousand dollars and a lawyer to verify your signature. I expect you to be here." Cord hurried down the walk. Pain or no pain, he couldn't spend one more moment in that man's presence, and hopefully, after tomorrow, he'd never have to see him again.

~

Cord pulled the letter for the sheriff from his pocket and set it on the desk. The guilt of paying Alda's father for her freedom still burned like a hot coal in his chest. If Cord hadn't been so desperate to get her out of prison, he would have stayed and tried to make the man see reason. He probably should have. How was he going to keep the transaction hidden from Alda?

Sheriff Dunn picked up the letter, and his eyes scanned back and forth across the page. "This letter is very detailed. I can't find any fault with what it says. Did you have any trouble getting her pa to sign it?"

Trouble? Other than paying the man a small fortune? "No, he seemed happy enough to do it." Judging by the glint that had been in Ira's eyes, it was all he could do not to jump in the air and kick his heels together.

"It's good to know we'll be able to let that girl go. She doesn't belong behind bars. I'll have a deputy send a telegram over to Laramie. She'll be able to leave as soon they get it."

"I appreciate it, Sir."

"Deputy Kenward says you're a bounty hunter. It's a bit unusual, isn't it? Making sure a wanted criminal goes free. Aren't you in the business for making money?"

"I don't figure she's a criminal."

"Taking anybody's mules without their say so, their pa's or not, is a crime. She's fortunate her pa was so understanding."

One thing Alda was not was fortunate, but he wasn't going to argue with the man setting her free. "You ever work with Sheriff Richards from Marysville?"

"Not directly, but he was known for good work. I was sorry to hear he passed."

"Sir?"

"We heard word a couple of weeks ago. His health took a turn for the worse, and he never recovered."

Heaviness settled into Cord's chest. He'd miss working

with Percy. The sheriff's pale face as he lay in his bed in the parlor struggling to talk on their last visit entered Cord's mind. Cord never did open the letter Percy had given him; he'd put it in his saddlebag and forgotten all about it. It should have some cash in it, too. Maybe he could send it to Percy's widow, Belle, as a condolence.

"Any chance you're the bounty hunter Sheriff Richards use to brag about?"

"If he did, he didn't brag to me."

"I suppose not, but rumor also has it the same hunter was responsible for turning in one of Doc Rufus's boys in Sidney. The capture caused quite a stir. Those three have been creating a lot of havoc."

"I guess I'm not as nameless as I thought I was."

"I'm not sure anyone knows your name, but they know what you look like. I'm assuming Doc and Emmet are looking for you, too."

"How's that?"

"They've been quiet since Owen died. Stands to reason they'd hold the man responsible for his capture also responsible for his death. We've had a couple of unconfirmed sightings in the area. I didn't put it together until now."

"Doc and Emmet have been seen around Cheyenne?"

"It's not always true. Folks can be odd that way, seeing a resemblance where there isn't any. However, the town's peppered with posters of the scoundrels. You better watch your back."

Cord would have to take care of Alda, before he could look into Doc and Emmet. "I'd better be going. I don't like the idea of Doc and his boy following me. When's the next train to Laramie?"

"The next one will leave at three o'clock this afternoon."

"That should give me time to fetch the mules. I was told your deputies rounded them and my horse up last week.

Where would I find them?

"Alda asked us to send them to Abney's Livery, and they've been asking about their bill. It's at the far end of Sixteenth.

"About my wallet, can I take it with me?"

The sheriff removed Cord's wallet from a drawer and handed it over. "You tell that girl to stay on the straight and narrow from here on in."

"I'll do my best, Sir."

Chapter Sixteen

Mrs. Snellen's severe face appeared at the bars on Rosie's and Alda's cell. Lifting a large ring of keys, she pressed one into the lock and opened the door. "Miss Alda Lealand, come with me."

Rosie's eyes brightened, and a smile spread across her face as she clutched Alda's arm. "Today could indeed be the day," she said.

"Mrs. Hazelwood, please desist from impeding Miss Lealand."

"You won't forget me, will you?"

"Rosie, perhaps I'm simply to be reprimanded for my insults toward the cook in the dining hall this morning." It would be heartless to encourage Rosie's fantasy of Cord's rescue. How would he even discover where Alda was?"

"Mrs. Hazelwood," Mrs. Snellen attempted to pry Rosie's fingers from Alda's arm. "I insist— "

"You're my only hope, Alda, you and your cowboy. Promise you won't forget me."

"I promise, if Cord rescues me, I won't forget you."

Rosie released Alda's arm, and Alda followed Mrs. Snellen's wide hips down the long corridor and past the rows of inmates. The catcalls and whistles no longer bothered her.

"Mrs. Snellen, could you tell me where we are going?"

"I've been asked to present you to the warden."

"The warden? Am I in trouble? Or is it about my court

date?"

"Miss. Lealand, please save your questions for the warden. I am not at liberty to give you any information."

Pa, I knew you could be cruel, but to leave me here, locked up, for the sake of your pride? Alda stifled a sob.

Mrs. Snellen led Alda through the heavy door at the end of the cell block and toward the warden's office in the central, two-story area of the stone building. The attractiveness of the prison belied the misery held within its walls.

Mrs. Snellen stepped to the side at the warden's door to allow Alda to enter the room. When Alda crossed the threshold, she faltered and her hands flew to her mouth. Cord rushed from his chair to steady her elbow.

Tears coursed down Alda's cheeks and over her fingers as she stared motionless at Cord. He'd found her. Cord had found her. Alda put her hands up to cover her head — her hair.

Cord stepped toward Alda and wrapped his arms around her shoulders. "Shhh," he whispered in her ear. "It's all right." He tucked her pitiful scarred head under his chin.

Alda closed her eyes and absorbed the rhythmic beat of Cord's heart as tears streamed down her face and dampened his shirt. If only she could stay here forever.

"Ahem," the warden cleared his throat.

Alda stepped away and hastily wiped the tears from her face with the back of her hands. "Yes, Sir."

"Miss Lealand, we have received notice from the sheriff in Cheyenne." He lifted a telegram from his desk. "The accusation against you has been dropped, and you are free to leave."

Alda turned toward Cord; moisture had gathered in his dark eyes. "My pa dropped the charges?" she asked.

He hesitated a beat before replying, "Yes, you are free."

"Thank You, Lord," Alda reached across the desk and took the warden's hands in her own. "Thank you, Warden," she said as she shook them. Alda turned to face Cord. "Thank you, too. Rosie knew you would come and find me."

Cord furrowed his brow. "Rosie?"

"Warden, Sir, would it be possible to go and say goodbye to Rosie, my cell mate? I'll only be a few moments."

"I'm sorry. We have found goodbyes between inmates to be more troublesome than beneficial. Mrs. Snellen can retrieve any items from your cell you wish to take with you. Mrs. Snellen?"

Mrs. Snellen stepped through the warden's office door. "Yes, Sir?"

"Would you please collect Miss Lealand's …" The warden looked toward Alda for her response.

She shook her head. "That's fine, Sir; I'll leave the few items I brought with me for Rosie. Where would I find my locket, sir, and Mr. Cord's wallet? I turned them in to the sheriff in Cheyenne."

"The sheriff has already returned my wallet, Sir."

"Mrs. Snellen, please retrieve Miss Lealand's locket from the safe and return it to her. I must get back to my work, so I will leave you in this gentleman's capable hands. I expect to not see you back here again, Miss Lealand."

Alda bowed her head. "Yes, Sir. Thank you again, Sir."

"I'm quite sure the only man you have to thank is the one standing next to you."

The only man? Alda glanced sideways at Cord. What about her pa? "Yes, Sir."

"Good day."

"Good day, Sir," Cord said, and slid his fingers around Alda's elbow.

Mrs. Snellen led the couple out of the room and asked them to wait while she obtained Alda's locket.

There were so many questions. Where were her mules? How did Cord find her? Why had her pa turned her in?

Where should she start? Alda looked over at Cord, and as his eyes met hers, her heart danced in her chest.

He grinned as she pulled at the few short spikes of hair on her head.

What had she been thinking to cut all her hair off? She must be a sorry sight.

"I can't say as I'm fond of your new hairstyle."

Shame burned its way up her chest, and Alda gave him what she hoped was a winsome smile.

"It was quite a shock seeing one of your curls on the deputy's desk."

"The deputy's? Back in Cheyenne? What was he doing with one of my curls?"

"He seemed rather attached." Cord reached into his breast pocket and pulled out one of her locks. "I rescued it. Would you like it back?"

Alda stared at the curl held together with a bit of green ribbon. For all the mischief her hair had caused her, it looked quite pretty in Cord's large hand. She raised her eyebrows as she asked, "Uumm, would you like to keep it?"

Cord's gaze traveled from her curl to her eyes and held. He looked like he wanted to ask her something.

"Yes?"

Mrs. Snellen's brisk steps interrupted the moment as she appeared with Alda's locket. Cord tucked Alda's lock back into his pocket as Alda took the necklace from Mrs. Snellen's extended hand and put the chain over her head. "Thank you for your kindness during my stay."

"I wish you well, Miss Lealand." Mrs. Snellen nodded curtly to both Alda and Cord and bid them goodbye.

Alda turned to speak. "Do you know where my mules are? I asked the deputy in Cheyenne to make sure Boss and the mules were taken care of. Did he send them to Abney's Livery?"

"Yes, I found all the animals quite happy. I arranged for

the mules and all your packs to be brought to Laramie with me on the train. They arrived safely and are waiting for you at the livery by the station."

"Thank you." Alda stepped with Cord through the doors of the prison where a black carriage waited on the wide graveled drive. The carriage wasn't the same as *Cord riding across a field on Boss,* but it served the purpose of Rosie's hopes just the same. "I haven't told you about my friend Rosie."

The driver of the carriage opened the door for Cord and Alda to board. Alda entered first and sat on one of the smooth benches. Cord winced as he ascended the carriage step.

"Your injury, I'd forgotten about it. Does it still hurt?"

Cord removed his hat, placed it on his knee, and took the bench opposite Alda. The carriage rolled down the road toward Laramie. "Every day it's a little better. It shouldn't be too much longer, and I will be back on my horse."

"And back to hunting criminals?"

Cord turned to stare out the carriage window for several moments as though lost in his own thoughts. "Yes," he shrugged, "back to hunting criminals." He turned toward Alda. "You were going to tell me about your friend."

"Rosie, yes, she's counting on you helping her."

"Counting on me? Why would she be counting on me?"

Alda's words came out in a rush, "I might have told her you liked to help people, and you were the most generous person I've ever met, and the kindness of your heart extended to innocent children, and I — "

Cord held his palm up and chuckled. "Quite the recommendation, but I'm not sure I'm all that."

"All that and more." Alda reached over to take Cord's hand and squeeze it briefly. "I also told her I knew you would help her once you heard her story."

"Ahhh. Would the help involve money by any chance?"

Alda studied the square of sunlight on the floor of the

carriage. "Yes, I'm afraid it will."

Quiet laughter spilled from Cord's throat, and then he leaned back and thumped the coach wall with the back of his head.

What was so funny?

"Is this perhaps what happens when a women sees the inside of a man's wallet?"

Alda opened her mouth to protest. What could she say? That she hadn't counted the seven thousand three hundred fifty dollars in Cord's wallet in the change room of the ladies wear store in Cheyenne. It was exactly what she'd done when she bought the new drawers. Drawers she wouldn't see again, thanks to Walker. "I admit, I counted the money. Why ever did you not put that amount of cash in the bank?"

Cord shrugged, "Sometimes I do, sometimes I … just don't concern myself with it. Looking back now, I probably shouldn't have been carrying that much money around." Cord's eyes glimmered with mischief. "It gives people the wrong idea."

Cord needed to hear Rosie's case. There was no way he wouldn't help her. "Please just hear the story first. I met Rosie on my third day at the prison. For the first two days, I didn't speak a word, I didn't eat. I was shocked — shocked that my pa would go so far as to turn me in. I wasn't the one who refused to sell the mules. I wasn't the one waiting for the big money to show up. And now, here I was, Wyoming Territorial Prison."

Cord stuck a finger in his collar and ran it from side to side although the coach wasn't overly warm.

"Are you feeling all right?" Alda asked.

"Mmm mm, go on."

"As I said, I wasn't the one who wasn't paying the county taxes, but I would be the one without a home. I still don't understand why he blamed me for doing what I did?"

Cord blew out a big puff of air and then held up his

palms, "I don't know. Maybe the man is too darn stubborn or maybe he thought you needed to learn a lesson. Or, perhaps he's a mean old rip who only cares about himself."

Alda tipped her head and stared at Cord. It almost sounded like he had met her pa. "I was broken hearted, and that's where Rosie comes in. She's not as old as my ma, but she reminded me of her. Rosie took me under her wing and asked Mrs. Snellen if we could be bunkmates. It's a good thing she did. I'd given up on my pa and …" Alda sniffed. "I honestly didn't think you would want to find me."

Cord moved to Alda's side of the coach and slid his hands over hers. "Why? Why didn't you think I would come and get you?"

Alda laid her head on Cord's shoulder. "Because I didn't deserve it. If my own pa didn't think I'm worth keeping out of jail, why would you? And now look at me." Alda lifted her head. Cord's face was a breath away. "Look at what I've done," she said, rubbing her hand over the angry tufts of red on her scalp.

Cord's eyes closed, and his lips lowered to hers. Alda pressed her hands against his chest. His arms went about her waist, and he gently explored the edges of her mouth with his own. A shiver coursed through her. She had hoped, prayed for this moment ever since seeing Cord in the hospital bed in Cheyenne. Alda returned Cord's seeking embrace.

Cord pulled away, put his forehead to hers, and whispered, "You will always be beautiful to me." And then he lifted his hand and ran his thumb along her jawline before taking her chin between his fingers. "Miss Alda Lealand, I love you."

Cord loved her. Looking as she did, temper and all, he actually loved her. "I love you, too," she said.

Cord smiled and leaned in to press his lips against hers once more before sitting back and lacing her fingers through his own. "Tell me more about your friend," he said

— his voice gravelly.

Alda wiped across her mouth with her sleeve. "Rosie knew the Lord, but she made a big mistake. Her husband left her for parts unknown several years ago and so she took in washing to feed her four children. The mayor's wife accidentally left a family heirloom brooch on one of the blouses sent to be laundered. Rosie found the brooch and had no intention of stealing it, but she couldn't resist borrowing it for a church function. She wore the brooch to a church supper. The mayor's wife didn't attend the church, but unfortunately her best friend did."

"Oh."

"The mayor's wife had no mercy for Rosie, and she landed in front of a judge. The judge couldn't find any evidence that Rosie intended to steal the brooch, but to keep peace with the mayor, he imposed a two hundred fifty dollar fine with incarceration until the fine is paid."

"And she can't work if she's in jail."

"She has no savings and two hundred and fifty dollars is more than half a year's wages for her. She's been in prison for over two months, and she's hoping and praying her oldest son is keeping the rest of the children fed."

"The deputy in Cheyenne said you were doing your share of praying, too."

Alda removed her hand from Cord's and smoothed the cotton of her mustard yellow skirt. "I think I finally found out what it means to trust in the Lord and to talk with Him. Thank you for sharing your faith with me."

"I didn't think I really said much," he shrugged.

"You didn't say a lot, but you said enough; and what's more, you lived it. It's only through prayer I knew I would still be all right if my pa didn't want me or," Alda swallowed, "if you didn't either." Alda clasped Cord's hand again.

"Rosie never gave up believing you would find me, though. She said before she even met me, the Lord gave her a dream about a cowboy riding a grey horse. I never told her about Boss; I thought it would be cruel." Alda giggled, "But here you are."

"How could I refuse to help a woman who dreams of me? I don't think there are many of them. Do you?"

"I, quite frankly, have no idea. I'm only aware of one."

"Only one?" he raised an eyebrow.

The corners of Alda's mouth turned up into a smile as she looked down at their entwined hands. "Perhaps two."

"I suppose, if there are so few of the species then, I should capitalize on the opportunity. You did say her husband left for parts unknown. I would also imagine the woman has a full head of hair."

"A beautiful head of hair in fact Mr., Mr. whoever you are, but I want to remind you that you told me I was beautiful no more than fifteen minutes ago. You can't go back on your word."

"Dearest, Alda, I will never go back on my word to you." His soft lips pressed against her forehead before he spoke again. "I'm assuming you want me to pay Rosie's fine so she can be released."

"Would you … please? Rosie expects to pay you back from her laundering money. It will take her some time to collect it, but I could also pay you from the sale of the mules. I'll have some money to spare after the property taxes. And then Rosie can pay me back." Alda cocked her head. "Now that I think about it, I'm surprised my pa didn't request the return of the mules if he was so angry. Although, I have no idea how he was going to come up with the money to save the farm."

"He must have had a change of heart."

"That's not like my pa."

Chapter Seventeen

Cord descended the step of the coach and rotated to help Alda. As she took his hand and exited, several onlookers at the train station gawked at them — most likely because of her missing hair. The only redeeming thought he could muster, looking at her hideous noggin, was the knowledge her hair would grow back. In the meantime, the sooner she found a bonnet amongst her packs — the better.

He was happy to be free of the coach. Although he enjoyed the closeness with Alda, and their shared kisses, her repeated questions about her father were becoming difficult to dodge. He still hadn't decided how to handle telling her the news of her father's negotiations. Nor had he decided when to put the ring in his pocket on her finger.

"Shall we see to the livestock? Where did you say the livery was? My trip from Cheyenne to Laramie is all a muddle. The poor deputy had to lead me around like a sheep," Alda said.

"Would you like to fetch a bonnet from your things first? The packs are in storage at the station."

"Why, Cord, I would almost entertain the notion that you don't long to be stared at. As you wish, I will find something to cover my poor head." Alda entered the station and returned ten minutes later wearing the same green bonnet she'd dropped in the dust the first day they'd met.

He reached up and tidied the bow under her chin. "I think this is my favorite one."

"I think it's my favorite, too." She slid her arm in his, and they walked companionably to the livery barn.

After entering Bessie's stall, Alda wrapped her arms around the mule and hugged her neck. "Bessie, I've so missed you and the others." She stepped back and patted the mule's withers. "She looks well; they all look well. Abney's has taken good care of them. They don't appear to be any worse off for the train ride over the pass either." Alda glanced down the row of wooden stalls. "Where's Boss?"

Cord leaned over the top rail of Bessie's stall to answer her. "He's back in Cheyenne."

Alda looked at him — her fine brows pulled together. "Back in Cheyenne? You haven't sold him have you?"

"I would never sell Boss."

"I don't understand. Are you sending me off alone with the mules? Are you leaving me?"

This wasn't going to be easy. "Yes, Alda, I'm sending you off alone."

"What?" Alda fell back against Bessie's shoulder. "Even after you kissed me? You said you loved me." Her voice faltered. "Was that some sort of cruel goodbye?"

"Listen, it's not like that."

Alda tugged Bessie's halter bringing the mule to the stall door. Cord stepped in front of her — blocking her exit

"Get out of my way," she said.

"No." He turned his palms toward her. "Just listen."

"Just listen to what? Some sorry excuse for why you can't really see a future for us as a couple. You should've given me the excuses before you said you loved me." Alda swiped at her eyes before untying the bonnet from her head and pulling it off. "I guess I don't need this anymore." The bonnet dropped to the muck of the stall. "Now get out of my way." Shouldering a path by Cord, Alda proceeded down the alleyway.

Cord stooped to rescue Alda's bonnet from the floor.

"It's Doc," he said to her back.

Alda's steps halted on the floorboards, and she rotated to face Cord slowly. "Doc Rufus and his son? You think you have to find them before you can go to California? They can't wait, is that it? Your job always comes first."

Cord exhaled before replying. "I think they've found me."

"How?"

"I didn't think anyone would recognize me in Sidney. I was never stationed there. Apparently someone did, though, and spread the news of my presence. Doc and Emmet must have heard the talk. They've been spotted around Cheyenne." He took a step toward her. "I am not willing to take a chance they catch up with both of us."

Alda nibbled at the edge of her lip. "I'm sorry. I always think the worst, but for the most part, I'm usually not that far off."

Cord couldn't stifle the chuckle rumbling from his throat.

"Let me go with you. I can shoot. Pa taught me how. Your injury's going to make you vulnerable; you need my help."

"I've arranged for a cattle car to take the mules to Daggett, California. It's the closest station to Death Valley."

"I know that; my uncle lives there when he's not hauling ore back and forth with the mule teams."

"It won't be difficult for you to find him then."

"Of course, it won't. He sent my ma the name of his boarding house, but I'm not going."

"Miss Alda Lealand, you are going."

Alda stomped her tiny boot. "I'm not going!"

"You're booked in the passenger car. You leave in two hours so I suggest we get moving. We have to load the packs, too."

"You're not listening. If I say I'm not going, I'm not

going."

The woman was as stubborn as one of her mules. "Alda, I know you mean well, but I would never forgive myself if I let you come with me and you got hurt. You don't want me broken do you, because that is what I'd be, a sorry excuse for a man, if something happened to you. Knowing you these few weeks has given me a hope for a future I actually want to be in."

"How do I know you'll make it?"

"You don't … and I don't … but God does."

Alda's gaze dropped to the floor. "So you're asking me to trust the Lord."

Cord closed the distance between them and wrapped his arms around her shoulders. "I'm asking you to trust the Lord. Whatever happens, it's His will. I promise you, though, I will do my best to come back to you."

"You better keep your promise," Alda said — her words muffled by the cotton of his plaid shirt.

~

Cord eased back on Boss's reins, and the horse slowed his pace. Rugged boulders of all shapes and sizes hugged the cliffs along the trail. Thick pine trees grew out of crevices in the rocks, aspens and wild roses mixed with the evergreens to create a lush forest. The eastern side of the Cheyenne Pass made for a steep climb. Boss had forded two crystal clear streams so far that morning, and Cord's canteen sloshed with the refreshingly cool water.

Cord's first journey through the Rockies would've been a whole lot more enjoyable if he wasn't a sitting duck. He'd made a fair production out of leaving town the day before. He had picked up foodstuffs he didn't need, considering the trip was only one day's hard ride, and he had asked several merchants for details about the pass. Most likely those same merchants would mention his questions to other folks.

Cord had made a point of making a few comments about his upcoming journey over the pass in the hotel dining room, too.

He missed Alda. Her tearful goodbye at the Laramie train station was almost enough to make him change his mind, but that would've been a foolish idea. The farther away she got from Doc and Emmett, the better.

It was hard to guilt the two of them if they were out for his blood, although Doc should assume some of the blame — him and his stupid pills. He probably figured death by poison ranked considerably higher than death at the end of a rope. Swinging sounded better to Cord.

Cord twisted his shoulders to relieve the tension building between them. It might be his imagination, but it seemed like the trees had eyes. If only he knew what the next few hours might bring.

A half mile down the trail, a loud pop sounded behind him. Sharp pain stung the top of his ear. He howled and rolled off the saddle — taking cover behind a jagged boulder. Boss dashed down the trail and out of sight — like he'd been taught.

Doc and Emmet must've gotten the message.

Cord's heart pumped hard. A trickle of warm blood ran down his neck. He felt for his ear. The rat had blown a slice clear off.

Cord pulled his Colt .45 from his holster. *Click, click, click, click.* "Doc! You gonna show yourself or shoot a man in the back."

Another *ping* and a shattered chunk of boulder flew into the air. Must be the latter.

Cord lay prone in the dirt as he surveyed his options: a steep bank, another boulder, a large pine.

Two to one didn't make for good odds. He scooted on his elbows behind the next boulder and peered out of the narrow crevice between them. No sign of Doc or Emmet — yet.

"Poster says dead or alive. I'd rather take you two in alive."

Ping. A sliver of rock shot into Cord's eye.

Argh. "Dang it." He pressed a finger into the corner of his eye and rubbed. *Kapow*. Cord let a shot go wild — buy some time until his sight cleared. "Doc, let me take you and Emmet in!"

Crack. Ping.

Cord ducked and slid then snaked his way up the backside of the pine. Here's hoping one of them was hot-headed. "Doc, you got Emmet set up with one of them pills, too? Owen cried like a baby after he swallowed it. Screamed for his mamma! Never heard such a caterwauling."

A branch quaked across the trail. Cord took aim with his good eye. *Boom*.

Whump. A body hit the ground.

"Is that two for two, Doc? I don't like taking a man's family."

Pop. Pop.

"Let me take you in, whoever you are."

Another shot rang out. "I ain't going nowhere with you."

Cord's chest constricted. Both boys were gone. What a waste of young life. He might have had a chance convincing Emmet to turn himself in if his pa was dead. Cord hated to be the one doing the killing. Better to leave that to the law.

Pop. Ping.

Four bullets before reload. Cord looked up. The branches would hold.

The forest held its breath, and Cord waited from above waited long enough for Doc to become curious and come looking.

One clear shot through the top of Doc's Stetson, and he was done for. He slumped to the ground never knowing what hit him.

Cord descended the tree hand over hand. His leg injury

made itself known, and he slid to the dirt below the pine. His left eye still hadn't cleared as he looked across the lush green valley. Rubbing at the missing chunk of ear, his fingers came away bloodied.

Never mind that Doc and his sons had taken the lives of women and children, snuffing out a man's life was never easy, nor was it safe. Bounty hunting was no life for a married man.

An image of Alda's pretty face, her hair intact, suspended itself across the valley. He couldn't bring her into his world; it wouldn't be fair. Cord pulled the diamond ring he'd purchased in Kansas City from his vest pocket and stared at it, then he rubbed the stone on his shirt several times, polishing it to a high shine, before tossing the ring over the rocks.

Ting, ting. The pretty solitaire that would've brought a beautiful smile to Alda's face bounced twice and disappeared into a crevasse.

Cord let out long, slow breath. He never should've gotten his hopes up, or Alda's either for that matter.

Boss wandered down the trail, meeting Cord as he sat on the dusty ground. He nuzzled Cord's shoulder with his lips before he nickered a greeting.

Cord reached up and wrapped his arm around the horse's neck. "You did good, ol' boy. It looks like it's going to be just you and me, again."

It took a couple of hours to find the other horses and load the bodies. The final quarter of the trail to Laramie narrowed to a wagon width. Cord didn't rush the journey nor did he enjoy the sights along the remainder of the pass.

The sheriff in Laramie was surprised to have the bodies of Doc and Emmet delivered to his door. Cord didn't bother to chat. He took the reward money and made a quick exit.

He'd spend a couple of nights in Laramie before taking the train to catch up with Alda. She deserved to hear directly why they couldn't be married. Cord wouldn't sneak off like her pa did.

Chapter Eighteen

Alda mopped her brow. The hot sun beat on her back, and she couldn't remove her bonnet. The week's train travel had covered most of the bald patches with fine red fuzz; however, it was no more appealing.

The mules complied as she led them from the cattle car at the Daggett Station to the livery barn. No doubt tired from the travel and the heat of the car.

She'd pared down her belongings along the way — sharing foodstuffs and provisions with those she met in the passenger car. Cord had given her enough money to stay in Daggett for a while if she chose. Once she found Uncle Larkin and sold the mules, there would be enough money to buy a ticket home, but going home wasn't near as appealing anymore.

Had Cord survived the encounter with Doc and Emmet? Had they even been looking for him? If Cord didn't show up in Daggett, she might never know. She could kick herself for not believing for sure if he would follow her.

Alda left the livery attendants with instructions for the mules before traipsing up Main Street. Nestled amongst the bald, desert hills, Daggett was a curious mixture of oddly shaped buildings, from tiny, wooden structures sporting tall, false fronts to low, stone buildings edged in brick.

The town bustled. Silver and borax mines in the vicinity bought men in to work and kept the train station busy shipping out ore.

Hopefully Uncle Larkin would be easy to find. The trip from the borax mines across the desert took several days, so it might take a few days for him to appear. Like she'd told Cord, he'd written Ma the name of his lodgings, Baxley Boarding House. Alda could leave word there.

She hadn't seen much of her uncle since he and her pa had parted ways. Larkin was known for his skill in training and working mules. He and her pa had invested together in the original draft mares and jacks. Bessie and her cohorts were a testament to his training.

He'd become frustrated, like her ma, with her pa's lack of business sense or common sense. Six Christmases ago, when there was no money for presents for Alda, Uncle Larkin had bought her the finest wooden sled in the county. She'd spent hours with her cousins sledding on the hills near their homes.

But it was the beginning of the end for the partnership. The two men had a row, and Uncle Larkin took off. He'd been mule skinning his way across the country ever since then. According to his letter to Mamma, Uncle Larkin's wages in Daggett were more than twice that of anywhere else at four dollars a day.

Alda entered a chophouse on Main Street and ordered two slices of turkey, mashed potatoes, and creamed spinach. No rice, no biscuits, and no bacon. It would be nice to see the last of those particular foods for some time.

The waitress directed Alda to the boarding house two blocks over. Alda knocked on the front door of a barn-red house with a row of matching rectangular windows across the second story. She took a deep breath as the shade of the wide veranda provided relief from the sweltering sun. An elderly woman answered her knock, her slight stoop a contrast to the pile of silver hair held fast by a tortoiseshell comb.

The woman glanced at Alda and began to close the door. "I don't take female boarders; try your luck at Faye's

Place down the way."

"I'm looking for my uncle."

The woman reopened the door and smiled. "You must be Alda."

"I am. It's nice to meet you …"

"Mrs. Baxley. Come in, child. Come in."

Alda followed her through the vestibule to the parlor.

With a slight tremor to her frail hands, she grasped Alda's. "I have been so looking forward to meeting you. Sorry to hear about your mother, dear. Your uncle has been telling us for weeks about how brave you are to bring your mules all the way to Death Valley by yourself. It's an absolute wonder."

"I started out by myself, but — "

"Do sit down." Mrs. Baxley indicated an intricately carved chair with green velvet cushions. "I'll find us some tea and cake." She tottered away leaving Alda to survey the fine furnishings in the room.

The delicate china vases and Queen Anne furniture did not look like they could withstand the rigors of a child, let alone her Uncle Larkin. Perhaps he had become more genteel since Alda had last seen him.

Mrs. Baxley returned several minutes later with a silver tray bearing a teapot, translucent teacups, and narrow slices of sponge cake.

Over tea, Alda shared the story of her journey; Mrs. Baxley clucked and patted her hand at the unsavory parts.

"And so you were put in jail by your own father? Mr. Lealand's brother?"

"One of our wagon team guides turned me in, but, yes, it was my pa who charged me with theft."

"It's so hard to believe Larkin's own brother would do such a thing. Larkin's such a kind and generous soul — always willing to help. He's done several repairs in my home without asking for any compensation. He's sure to drive me to church every Sunday, too."

"My Uncle Larkin drives you to church?" Uncle Larkin had never been a church going man.

"He picks up several of us widows. I must say, his singing voice is a veritable asset to our small congregation."

"He sounds like he's found his place here."

"He has; as long as the borax mine holds out, he'll have work and a home. He's due to be back today. If you go down to the train station in the next hour or so, he will be pulling in with one of the mine wagons. They are a sight to see. He will be so happy to know you've arrived safe and sound. Although what he'll think about his brother, I'm not quite sure."

"I'll take my leave and go to the train station then. It was nice to meet you. Thank you for the wonderful treat. It's been a while since I've tasted anything so delicious."

"Be sure to come back and visit before you leave town."

Alda broke a sweat the moment she stepped off the veranda. Missouri never warmed to the temperatures of the desert.

It was a wonder Uncle Larkin had tamed in Daggett. Pa never mentioned any religious upbringing. Maybe Uncle Larkin had found the Lord on his own. It would be a pleasure to go to church with family if she was still here on Sunday. Her ma's crestfallen expression every time Alda refused to attend church on a Sunday morning hadn't pained her then, but it did now. If only she could take those years back. The years since she was a little girl and refused to go because her pa said only the weak needed the church.

As Alda neared the train station, the tallest wagon she'd ever seen in her life, pulled by a pile of mules, was parked alongside a rail car. She heard a *whoop* and a whistle before a lanky form descended from the wagon. Alda would've recognized the dusty face and shock of dark hair standing on end anywhere.

"Alda? Is that you, sweetheart?" Uncle Larkin pulled her into his arms and rubbed his stubbled chin on her cheeks like he had when she was a little girl.

Alda pulled from his embrace and straightened her bonnet. "Uncle Larkin, please, I'm a grown woman now."

He put his outstretched hands on her shoulders. "Let me take a look at you, girl. Miss Alda Lealand, I believe you are right; you are a grown woman. How did it happen? I just saw you a year or two ago."

"Uncle Larkin, you haven't been back home for six years."

"Six years? How is that possible?" He lifted his battered hat, and a cloud of dust puffed up from the fingers scratching his scalp. "Sorry to hear about your ma, child. I'd always admired Julia. Your aunt was kind enough to let me know."

"Thank you. I know she admired you, too."

"I could never quite figure out what she saw in my brother, but that's a whole nother story. Now climb up here on the wagon with me while the men unload. Isn't she something?"

Uncle Larkin hoisted Alda up on one of the giant wheels. "From up here, I feel like I can see clear across the desert. These wheels alone are seven feet high and weigh a thousand pounds each."

Alda reached up to steady herself with the wagon's edge. "These boxes must be solid to carry all the weight."

"They're solid oak," he smacked the side of the box, "and made to last."

"How much weight are the mules pulling?"

"The wagon empty is about eight thousand pounds. The mules haul thirty-seven tons in one train."

"Thirty-seven tons?" The mule team fidgeting in front of the wagon didn't look like they could pull thirty-seven tons.

"We've never lost a single animal, and we've never lost

a load. I can't say the same about the mule skinners, though, but that had to do with some bad choices they made."

"I can't say the same either. I lost Charlie on the way."

"Good old Charlie?"

"We landed in one of those frightening prairie thunderstorms not far from Marysville. The string got worked up, and Charlie strangled on his lead in the mayhem. It shouldn't have happened; I should have been watching the weather more closely."

"I'm sorry to hear it, but I'm sure you did your best. Charlie was always a little on the skittish side. Did you notice the wheelers here are horses? It's called a twenty-mule team, but it's really only eighteen — two teams of nine mules."

"Well, I've only got eight left. You'll have to find another mule to finish out the team. Do you think our mules can pull this much weight, though?"

"Your mules can pull this much and then some. There's nothing quite like the Missouri Mule, and ours were the best. I haven't seen anything out here to match them. That's what made me so frustrated with your pa. We always had a superior product that could've made us both a lot of money. I'm surprised you and your ma convinced him to finally sell."

So here it was, the discussion she fervently hoped would never happen. It was probably easier than facing her pa, though. "He didn't know."

"What?" Uncle Larkin's head snapped up. "He didn't know? You mean you took off with some of your pa's prize mules without asking him?"

"It was either that or lose the farm. Mamma knew he wouldn't sell, and you mentioned in your letter mules sell for twice their value here. That's how we came up with the plan, if you can call it a plan. It was more like an escape. Pa left for Excelsior Springs just a few days after the funeral.

Three days later, I took the opportunity to get out of town. I left the neighbor with the responsibility of taking care of the animals. I also told the neighbor he could give Pa the bill for his services when he returned. Just because I work for nothing, doesn't mean the neighbor should."

Uncle Larkin sucked air between his teeth and his tongue like he had when he was contemplating what to say.

Alda waited for him to string his thoughts together.

"Can't say as I'm too happy with this situation."

"Larkin, are you going to keep this poor girl talking in the hot sun all afternoon? I can see she's nigh on melting already."

Alda drew the sleeve of her dress across her sopping brow before looking down toward the squeaky voice. A whip of a boy, about fifteen, with deep brown curls and a white slice of a smile looked up at her.

"Newton, you go on now. This is my niece I've been telling you about."

"You're the girl who drove a pack string clean across the country?" Newton climbed onto the wheel axle and reached out his hand. "I sure am glad to meet you."

Alda laughed as she bent down to shake the grimy fingers stretching her way.

"Just a second," Newton said and scrubbed at his dusty pants with the flat of his hand. Then he offered up a hand which was just as grimy the second time.

"Nice to meet you, but I wouldn't want you to get the wrong impression." Alda glanced over at her uncle. "The mules and I have spent the last week in the cars. We left Laramie, Wyoming, only a week ago."

Uncle Larkin looked like he was doing some more figuring. "Newton's right; the sun's too hot out here to keep talking. I'll take you up to the Stone Hotel and buy you a lemonade."

"You including me in that invite, Larkin? I don't mind admitting I'm parched. We come through some hot sun today."

"Newt, you know I can't keep you from your job. You get those mules unharnessed and rubbed down."

"And no lemonade?"

"Buy yourself some, boy, if you want. You make good money."

Alda and Uncle Larkin traipsed up the dusty street, leaving Newt to complain about mule skinners' lack of appreciation for swampers and their contribution to make the job smoother for both of them.

"Would you like to look in on the mules on our way? They're here at the livery," Alda said.

"Let's do that. I've been missing those beasts. The mine foreman was pretty excited when I told him I had a first-rate team on the way."

"I don't think they've changed much. I might have two or three you've never worked with, but the others you'll know. I couldn't have asked for better company. Other than a couple of them taking off across the prairie on my second night out, and of course losing Charlie, I didn't have any trouble."

Both sets of doors on the livery barn were open, allowing a warm breeze to drift from one end to the other. As Alda and Uncle Larkin stepped into the shadows of the barn, the mules raised their heads and peered over the rail of their stalls.

Uncle Larkin slapped his leg and let out a shout. "No. Is that Moses?" He scratched the mule between the ears. "You old thing. How'd you make a trip, and that far? Even halfway at that."

Moses pulverized the hay in his mouth; his doleful eyes stared clean through Uncle Larkin and Alda.

"Arthur ... and Gideon ..." Uncle Larkin bounced from stall to stall. "Bud ... Old Joe. You've put together a superior team, Alda. I can see why they were so dependable." He stopped to let Bessie sniff his hand.

The mule nickered like she remembered who he was. That was Bessie, the smartest mule ever born.

"You think so? I thought they might work well together, but you never know until you're out on the trail. We don't need teams of nine or eighteen at home."

"You did a fine job, but what's your pa going to say when he finds out? He's going to think I was in on the whole thing, and we've got enough bad blood between us."

"He's found out already. I know exactly what he's going to do." Alda's heart pounded a beat just talking about it. "He's going to charge me with horse theft and have me put in jail."

"Hey now, sweetheart," Uncle Larkin put his arm around Alda and pressed, "I might not appreciate everything my brother does, but I don't think he'd stoop as far as putting his own flesh and blood in jail."

Alda pulled out of Uncle Larkin's embrace to face him. "Well, I do know, and that's exactly what he did."

"Ira went to the law?"

"Thanks to my pa, I spent ten days in Wyoming Territorial Prison."

"Is that why your pretty curls are gone?"

Alda put her hand up on her bonnet. "You can tell?"

"I've known you your whole life and how hard it is for you to tame that unruly mop of red. I can tell when it's not there."

Alda exhaled "I picked up a case of fleas from the blanket in my first cell in Cheyenne. And then I got carried away with a neighbor's knife. My pa loved my hair, but I guess he didn't love me near as much."

"Come here." Uncle Larkin wrapped her up in a bear hug, and Alda sniffled into his chest. "I have to admit, this is a new low for your pa. How did you get out?"

"The story's a long one. I can tell you over the lemonade."

When they arrived at the lobby of the Stone Hotel, Alda

tipped her head back and turned in a circle. She held her arms aloft from her body to balance while she stared through the large glass dome above the second story.

"It's a wonder, isn't it? This hotel was built last year, and the walls are two feet thick. That's what keeps it cool. People come from all over to stay here. The heat of the desert can get to you after a while."

"I've never seen anything like it — the blue sky behind the dome looks like an enormous sapphire."

Uncle Larkin pulled the ornate wrought iron handles on a heavily carved door and motioned for Alda to precede him. "The dining room sells fresh squeezed lemonade that can cut the thirst of a day across the sand. I come here often. Newt waggles his way in when he can. He sends most of his money back home. His parents have twelve mouths to feed so he doesn't like to spend his own money if he can help it."

Alda and Uncle Larkin were shown to a booth in the dining room. "You care for anything else, besides two cold lemonades?" the waitress asked before eyeing Alda up and then tacking on an arrogant smile.

"Lemonade will be fine for me; I just finished my lunch," Alda said.

The waitress cocked her head to the side and gave Uncle Larkin a saucy look. "Anything else for you, Preacher Larkin?"

"Lemonade will be all, Miss Cora. Thank you."

The exaggerated sway of the woman's hips was a wonder to watch as she went to fetch their lemonades. "Is there something I should know about the waitress? She appears a bit … peeved at me, or maybe you — I'm not quite sure."

He removed his dusty hat and put it on the bench next to him. "I haven't always been what you could call 'circumspect' in this town." He cleared his throat.

Was that a blush making its way up her uncle's neck?

She'd never seen one on him before. With all the sand and sweat plastered to his skin, it was hard to tell.

"When I first arrived, I went a little wild with all the spare cash. Cora and I, we … uh…"

It was definitely a blush. Alda reached out her hand to pat her uncle's. "I understand what you are trying to say. There's no need to give me the details."

Uncle Larkin's face relaxed. "I've changed my ways, Alda. One of the other mule skinners pestered me to go to church with him, and I finally went. I can't tell you how much I enjoyed hearing the Word and praising with those people. It felt like a heavy load was lifted off my back."

"Mrs. Baxley told me you give rides to her and several other widows."

"So you met my landlady. The woman spoils me rotten. Every Sunday, I take her and a few of her widow friends to church."

"She also said she enjoyed your singing voice."

"Did she? It takes me back, the singing. It reminds me of when your pa and I were little boys. Our mamma, your grandmother, used to trot us to the front of the church and have us belt out hymns for the rest of the congregation."

"You and my pa went to church?"

Cora arrived with their lemonades and put a frosted glass with a wedge of lemon tucked onto the rim in front of each of them. Alda's sloshed over the side, leaving a small puddle around the base of her glass.

As Cora turned to leave, Uncle Larkin spoke, "Miss Cora, I'd like you to meet my niece all the way from Missouri, Miss Alda Lealand."

Cora beamed her first genuine smile. "Your niece? Well, why didn't you say so?" She extended her hand to shake Alda's. "Nice to meet you," she said and wiped the puddle up with the small towel pulled from her waist.

"Nice to meet you, too."

Cora's hips did considerably less swaying as she left to

serve other customers.

"My pa never mentioned going to church when he was little."

"When he was about ten, he refused to go anymore."

About the same age Alda was when she told her mamma her church going days were over. Maybe she had more of her pa in her than she liked to admit. "Why did he stop going?"

"He just repeated what he'd heard our own pa say 'Religion's only for the weak; he's a self-made man.' You know what I'm talking about. You've heard it your whole life."

She had heard it her whole life. Even sadder still, she'd believed it. "What about you, Uncle Larkin? When did you stop going?"

"I was different from your pa. I didn't hold anything against the church. I drifted away. I let the pursuit of money overtake me, and I forgot about the Lord. That's changed now. Sure I still make money, but it's not all I live for."

"I can tell you're different. I am, too." Alda took a sip of her lemonade. The tart liquid cooled the back of her throat.

"Are you saying what I think you're saying?"

"I met someone on the trail. He told me God just wanted me to love Him back. For a while, I traveled with a wagon train with a preacher along, too. He showed me lots of verses about God's love for me. It's what I needed to hear, that God wasn't like my pa. I surrendered my life to Jesus, God's Son."

Uncle Larkin gripped her fingers. "Alda, it makes me so happy to hear that. You've been in my prayers, especially since your ma said you'd be coming this way."

Was that why it seemed like the Lord was with her? And why He kept putting people who loved Him in her path? The thought warmed her insides.

"So who was it?"

"Who was what?"

"The fellow you met on the trail who told you about God's love. The fellow who makes your eyes go all soft when you bring him up."

"His name's Cord. He rescued me from a few," Alda pursed her lips, "situations, I guess you could call them. He's the one who got me out of jail, too. He had some unfinished business in Cheyenne, Wyoming, and it was dangerous. I'm hoping and praying he'll show up in Daggett in the next day or two."

"I'll add my prayers to yours, Alda."

Chapter Nineteen

If only Cord could have a photograph of Alda's face when he slipped onto the backless bench beside her during the church service. Her initial look of astonishment, which filled with pure delight, was enough to start his heart thumping right out of his chest. She looked like a china doll in her pretty sky blue dress and straw hat. He couldn't resist a quick squeeze to her hand before leaning forward and nodding to the man on her left who returned his greeting. The man must be her Uncle Larkin, although there sure wasn't much resemblance to her feisty little pa.

The small schoolroom serving as a church was filled with men of all ages and older women.

The room settled again, and the pastor spoke, "Please turn in your Bibles to John, Chapter fifteen, beginning with verse five, 'I am the vine, you are the branches …'"

Now that he was here, with Alda fidgeting beside him, the idea of telling her they didn't have a future as a married couple seemed like a cruel thing to do. It would've been better to have just gone his way and not followed her to Daggett — drifted out of her life like some kind of forgotten memory. Cord forced his attention back to the pastor's words.

"'If you abide in me, and my words abide in you, ask whatever you wish, and it will be done for you,'" the pastor continued.

When the service finally ended, Alda jumped up.

"Cord, when did you arrive? I am so happy to see you …" She took a sharp breath.

"Alive?"

"Yes," Alda wrung her hands together, "alive. How did you find us?"

"I asked at the train station if there was a church service in town and took a chance you would be here."

"You must be Cord, the one Alda's told me so much about," the man who'd been sitting next to her said.

Alda stepped back so the two men could shake hands. "Yes, Cord, this is my Uncle Larkin. Uncle Larkin, Cord … uhh."

Uncle Larkin raised his thick eyebrows and leaned forward.

"Sweet, Sir. Cordell Sweet."

Alda tipped her chin and mouthed his name as though considering if it wore well on him or not. Why had he kept it a secret from her so long?

An elderly woman joined their circle. "Are you Cord?" she warbled. "The one who rescued Alda?"

Cord sought Alda's gaze. Was he her rescuer? Perhaps with Felix, but she wouldn't have been in prison if he hadn't let down his guard with Walker. "I think Miss Alda has rescued me as many times as I've rescued her."

"He's only being kind, Mrs. Baxley. Yes this is Cord, Cord Sweet." Alda threw him a quick smile.

The elderly woman touched the edge of his suit sleeve. "It's so very nice to meet you. I hope you will join us for a roast beef dinner at my home."

Cord's mouth watered at the words. The hit and miss meals on the journey from Laramie had left him famished most of the time. "I would be happy to."

With Alda's uncle leading Mrs. Baxley by the arm, they made their way through the groups of people visiting and out to the exterior door.

Victoria? There was no mistaking the statuesque blond

swathed in lilac ruffles standing on the schoolhouse lawn. As Victoria rushed toward Cord, Alda's brow furrowed, and she scooted over beside her uncle and Mrs. Baxley. The cloying perfume he'd always hated assailed Cord's nose in the cloud created by Victoria's ruffles.

"My dearest Preston, I have missed you so much." Victoria's arms shook as though she was overcome by emotion.

It was only an act; her nerves were made of steel. He pulled himself out of her embrace and held her at arm's length. She'd grown even more beautiful since they'd last seen each other two years ago. She'd always owned the title of neighborhood sweetheart, but maturity had brought her the gift of being truly gorgeous. "Victoria, what are you doing here?"

"Preston, are you not happy to see me?"

Happy? No, it wasn't happiness he was feeling. If Victoria found him, then Hayden must have found him — and that meant Cord's father knew where he was.

"Excuse me," Mrs. Baxley said, "we haven't met, but we've invited Mr. Sweet for lunch. Would you care to join us?"

Victoria brought her splayed fingers to her neck. "I'm not sure. I thought perhaps Preston and I would — "

He deserved the confused looks at the name of Preston. There was no reason Alda should take him seriously ever again. "Victoria would love to join us, Mrs. Baxley. I'll make formal introductions when we arrive. Where do you live?"

"Just down the block, the only red house on the right hand side."

"Alda, would you care to wa — "

"I'll catch a ride with my uncle, thank you … Preston." Alda turned on her heel and strode away.

Judging by the lilt in her step, she was angry. It would take some doing to sort this sorry mess out.

Uncle Larkin bobbed his head. "We'll see you both shortly."

Victoria wound her arm through Cord's as they turned to walk up the street. "Preston, why did you tell those people we would share a meal with them? We have so much catching up to do. Let me take you to lunch. We can stop by, if you like, and give our regrets." Victoria removed a lace fan from her bag and vigorously fanned her cheeks. "The temperature in this place is enough to make me swoon. Why ever did you come here?"

"I arrived this morning; and you, when did you arrive?

"I came in from Los Angeles yesterday. I'm staying at the Stone Hotel, a quaint place. You can take a room there, too."

"So Hayden finally caught up with me." The man was relentless when his father convinced him something needed to be done.

Victoria tapped his arm. "My dear, Hayden's been closing in for some time. It's quite exciting for the rest of us — regular telegrams about where you might be headed next. He finally caught up with you in, hmmm, let me think, Lo — "

"Laramie?" How had he not been killed before if a butler could chase him down?

Victoria laughed the melodic yet hollow laugh she used when she didn't mean it. "Yes, Laramie. Hayden said he only caught up with you because you returned. Daddy was proud to learn you brought in a couple of fugitives from the law."

Leave it to his father to be proud of one of the most miserable days of Cord's life. "I'm sure he was," Victoria didn't flinch at his sarcasm. "Why did he send you, Victoria? He told me I was to never darken his door again."

"You're so full of pride, just like Father. The two of you make it difficult for us womenfolk."

Victoria's mincing was getting annoying. "Cut it out; I

know you're not delicate."

"All right, I can live without the constant comparisons to the decorated Preston Cordell Sweet, but Mother has cried herself to sleep every night since you left. Father finally relented and said you could come home. I think Mother had Hayden's bag packed before he finished speaking. Apparently," Victoria's fan snapped shut, "Mother's aspirations for me are not enough to keep her happy." Victoria reached up and pinched the side of Cord's cheek.

Cord rubbed at the spot where his sister had pinched him.

Victoria pinched his other cheek. "She needs her little Preston."

This was the Victoria he knew.

"Father sent me to convince you to come home. Between the three of us, he thinks I have the most influence over you." She looked at him from the corner of her eye. "But we both know you only do what you want to do, don't we?"

"Speaking of only doing what you want, I see there's no wedding ring on *your* finger. Have you not been cooperating with Mother's plans either?"

"Cooperating? You're one to judge, Preston. How could I cooperate with the simpering line of potential suitors she's invited for dinner parties. They drone on and on about paltry bits of boring business they've attended to. I have feigned a sudden stomach ailment more times than I care to count."

"Perhaps you are the reason Mother's crying herself to sleep."

Victoria picked up the edges of her skirt to step onto the sidewalk leading to Mrs. Baxley's home. "Even if I was, you can carry the blame for that, too. I learned to escape her designs on my life from the best."

Victoria's stiff smile and steeled look reminded him of

the times she'd faced their father, demanding something expensive like a new cart for her pony or the latest dress design from Europe. "Don't you think Mother deserves at least one of her children to fall in with her plans?"

"Then you do it," she said and stalked up to Mrs. Baxley's porch.

That was not going to happen.

The scent of cooked roast beef welcomed them as Alda opened the door. She wore a lacy white cap. Perhaps Mrs. Baxley had found it for her and considered it less offensive than Alda's shorn head. He chuckled inwardly at the escaped tufts of red jutting along the cap's edge. His gaze dropped to her face. She looked unhappy.

"Do come in." Alda indicated the parlor door behind her. "Mrs. Baxley is supervising the finishing of the meal. I'll bring you some tea."

Victoria handed her hat and bag to Alda and strode past her dismissing her as one of the staff. Alda stared at the hat and bag in her hand for a moment as though she didn't know what to do with them.

Cord touched her shoulder.

Alda startled.

"I'm sorry, Victoria can be quite … officious." When Alda looked up at him, his breath hitched. She looked like a lost child. He wanted to wrap her up in his arms and tell her he would help her through whatever was bothering her. But it wasn't true. He never should've come to Daggett.

"Preston, are you coming to join me?"

"Alda, come and let me introduce you."

Alda winced and then nibbled at the edge of her lip. "Uuhhm. I'll fetch the tea and meet you in the parlor," she said and bolted down the narrow hallway.

He crossed to the parlor. Victoria held a delicate figurine of a cupid with tiny purple wings in her hand. A matching figure sat atop the fireplace mantle.

"Preston, isn't he exquisite? I don't think I've seen one

quite so detailed before. I must ask Mrs. Baxley where she found it." Victoria turned the figure on end to look at the base. "That's not any help, only an x."

Cord took the figure from his sister's hand. "You shouldn't be picking up the ornaments. What if you broke one?" The tiny cupid held a scroll with the words *marriage contract* in fancy black lettering. He traced a pointer finger over the words.

"Preston, you don't seem quite like yourself." Victoria glanced down at the figure in his hand and back up to his face.

Cord's neck heated up, one of the indications a line of red was making its way up his face. He'd never been able to keep a secret from Victoria. If he tried, she would fill in the missing bits herself, and then he was really in trouble. "I fell in love." There, he'd said it. The family could do with the declaration as they pleased.

"You fell in love? My brother, Preston Cordell Sweet, fell in love? After all the years Mother paraded you and Henriette around to our family and friends and Mother thinking she'd struck gold when Henriette's father finally agreed the two of you could marry."

"I don't need to be reminded." Henriette had never tugged at his heart — not like Alda, from the moment he first met her.

"Not every family is worth the millions they are."

"I never cared about the money."

"Perhaps not, but I don't understand. You never claimed to love Henriette, and you were almost married."

"You know I had little to do with that scenario. Mother should've never gotten involved." If he hadn't left home when he did, his mother would've convinced him to marry Henriette eventually — love or no love. Cord set the cupid on the mantle next to its match.

"Who is the lucky woman?"

"Miss Alda Lealand." She was by no means lucky

though.

"Is she here? Can I meet her?"

"You've met her already, briefly."

Victoria pulled her eyebrows together in a deep vee. "I've already met her? When?"

"I assume you thought she was the maid, the young woman from the church who answered the door."

"What, the tiny spit of thing with some sort of disorder?" Victoria plucked at the edge of her hairline.

"She doesn't have a disorder." Telling Victoria Alda cut her hair off in prison wouldn't help. "It's a long story," he said.

"Are you engaged to be married?"

Cord exhaled. "No, we're not. Alda and I are not getting married."

Teacups rattled, and Cord turned to see Alda's dress disappear around the corner of the parlor door.

Victoria clutched his arm. "Preston, let her go."

Cord pulled at Victoria's fingers to pry them off of his arm. "What do you mean let her go? She wasn't supposed to find out this way."

"Then don't make it worse by chasing after her."

"How would I be making it worse?"

"Did you ever actually propose to Alda?"

"No," but he had tossed the notion back and forth in his mind for weeks trying to find a way to marry her and have some sort of a life together, "not really."

"Then any presumption on her part is precisely that, presumption. She'll only feel more embarrassed if you hunt her down — her face a wreck of tears," Victoria's volume rose, "and try to explain something that didn't happen in the first place."

He stared at his sister. "Victoria, are you talking about yourself or Alda?"

Uncle Larkin stuck his nose through the parlor archway. "Are you folks all right in here?"

Straightening his shoulders and drawing the edges of his jacket together Cord spoke, "Not really, Sir. I've hurt Alda." He narrowed his eyes toward Victoria to warn her to keep quiet. "If you wouldn't mind finding her, I would like a few moments to speak with her, and then we will take our leave."

"So you're not sticking around for the roast beef dinner?"

"I'm sorry, we won't be able to."

Uncle Larkin scratched at the side of his head. "I'll go and find Alda then," he said, and his footsteps retreated down the hallway.

"Preston, listen; let's just slip out. We don't need to stay here. If there are no trains leaving tonight, we can catch a coach to the nearest town and leave for home tomorrow."

"I need to talk to Alda. I can't let her down like this. I can't be like her father and I'm not going home!"

"What do you mean you're not going home?"

"I am not going home with you."

"What are you saying? I've come all this way. It took Hayden months to find you. What about Mother?" Victoria squared her shoulders. "You *are* coming home with me."

"I'm a grown man, with my own life." So what if it wasn't perfect. "I've been praying about it for weeks, and I've finally forgiven father for banishing me from our home. I now realize it was for the best, and the Lord's not asking me to return. I won't live out Mother and Father's designs for my life."

"Sorry to interrupt. I thought I should let you know Alda's not here," Uncle Larkin said.

"Do you know where she went?"

Uncle Larkin shook his head. "I don't. She must have sneaked out the back door. Probably didn't go far. You might find her at the hotel. It's the Daggett on Main."

"Thank you." Cord moved toward the door. "Victoria,

go home."

Victoria followed him, pleading. "Let me help you find her, and then we can talk."

"I don't want your help. If you ever want to see me again, you will leave Daggett, and you will leave *now*."

"Preston, please."

"I promise you, I will pay the family a visit before the year is out. Give Mother and Father my regards."

The screen door snapped shut as Cord jogged across the veranda and onto Mrs. Baxley's lawn. He ignored the spike of pain shooting up his thigh.

A little more than half an hour later, Cord sat on the bed in his hotel room. The inquiry at Alda's hotel had yielded no results. They hadn't seen her since she left for church that morning.

He stared out the window over Scott's Market and toward the sage-covered foothills. Where would Alda go? Where could she go? There wasn't much to Daggett, and now that the mules were sold, she could jump on the train or in a coach. She probably already had.

Cord's stomach kinked at the thought, and he hung his head. He didn't deserve a farewell, not after what she'd heard in the parlor. There was no way they could become man and wife, but to never see her pretty smile or contend with her banter… ever again? He groaned and punched the mattress.

Falling to his knees, he bent forward in prayer. "Lord, this morning I heard Your Word. You said if I abide in You, and Your words abide in me … Lord, I've been abiding in You, and I've been reading Your Word. And You said ask, Lord, so I'm asking. I need Your help. I love Alda. I love her like I've never loved anyone. How can we be together? Military or bounty hunter, neither are any kind of a life. But I can't take the pain. If this is what it feels like to be without her, Lord, I can't do it. Show me a way, please."

Cord rose from the floor and removed his suit. He donned his usual garb of denim waist overalls and cotton shirt. It wouldn't hurt to ride Boss around town and ask about Alda. The horse would appreciate getting out of his stall and stretching his legs.

Picking up his saddlebag from the floor, he opened the flap. One of the handkerchiefs Alda had insisted on buying him in Laramie was tucked in between his ammo and a spare shirt. He tugged on the corner of the red cotton. The letter Sheriff Richards gave him in Marysville tumbled out of his bag and onto the floor, unopened. Alda hadn't wanted to split the money.

She was probably wishing she had now.

Was everything going to remind him of that girl?

Cord tore open the top of the envelope. Inside were two fifty dollar bills and a sheet of notepaper. Cord stuffed the money in his pocket. He could look into wiring the money to Sheriff Richards' widow tomorrow when the bank opened.

Unfolding the notepaper, he read the words on the page.

Dear Cord,

> My wife is writing this letter for me as my hand won't stop shaking. If you read this right after you leave, there's a chance I might still be alive, and you can come back and ask me your questions. If you don't, and I suspect that might be the case, then there's a good chance I've gone on to glory. I will meet you there after a long life providing you take my advice and stop putting yourself in so much danger.
>
> You are good at what you do, and the law needs men like you. I've asked the city of Marysville to take you on as my replacement. It's a little unorthodox; however, it didn't take much

convincing. You have become a legend in our part of the country on account of your bounty hunting exploits. Thanks to your friend's photograph, we also learned you were a decorated soldier.

I'm hoping you are ready to give up the life of a bounty hunter and settle down. If so, the Marysville Sheriff's Office looks forward to continuing the battle against the criminal element under your leadership.

Sincerely,

Percy Richards

Chapter Twenty

Alda gulped lemonade from a tall glass. When she'd run through the double doors of the Stone Hotel dining room, Cora had taken one look and directed her to the linen closet. She had upended a crate and ordered Alda to sit. Several moments later, Cora had returned with the lemonade.

Cora's eyes went as round as silver dollars when Alda pulled off her straw hat, but she didn't say a word.

Alda set the glass down on the nearby shelf and fished in her pocket. "How much do I owe you?"

"This one's on me. I thought you might faint away when you ran through those doors. Are you looking for Larkin?"

"No, I was looking for…" What was she looking for — a place to hide? "I don't know what I was looking for. I need to spend some time alone right now."

"I know man troubles when I see them. You take all the time you need. The housekeeping staff has gone home for the day so no one will disturb you. I'll come and check on you later."

"Thank you."

The latch clicked as Cora closed the door to the narrow room filled with shelves of linens and cleaning supplies. Alda had been a fool to think Cord, Preston, whoever he was, had intended to marry her. And why would he when he could have the likes of the woman in Mrs. Baxley's parlor? She was striking, tall, and slender. Judging by her clothes, she was well off, too.

How could Alda even begin to compare? Some had thought her cute. When they said it, though, it was like they were talking about a pet. Cord was the only man who ever called her beautiful. Alda kicked the crate with the back of her heel. He hadn't meant it, but she had believed him.

She thought back to their ride in the coach from the prison. When had he ever said he would marry her? The kisses they'd shared seemed real, and then he'd said he loved her. But not once had he ever said he intended to marry her. The notion had been Alda's, and a fool's notion at that.

Cord proved to be like her father. He held a dream in front of her — a dream he had no intention of fulfilling because something better might come along. And she'd fallen for it without question — when she should have known.

Alda's whole body grew heavy with the pain of Cord's betrayal. As she rocked on the crate, she brought her hands to her face to catch the tears streaming from her eyes. Alda cried until the tears dampened the yolk of her dress and soaked the cuffs of her sleeves.

When her breaths slowed, she waited a few moments and then lifted the hem of her petticoat and dried her face.

Cord was right about one thing; she could count on the Lord. She could always count on the Lord.

Her business in Daggett was done. Uncle Larkin had mentioned receiving payment from the mine for the mules on the way to church. If she picked up the money, she could get out of town by train or coach, whatever it took, and make her way home.

Most likely Cord and his woman friend would have left Mrs. Baxley's by now. Alda stood, shook out the folds of her skirt, and replaced her hat. She would thank Cora for the drink then go and talk to Uncle Larkin.

Alda opened the door to the linen closet and peered through the crack. The woman from Mrs. Baxley's was stomping down the hallway, her hat askew, with a line of sweat trailing down the back of her dress. Lovers' spat perhaps? Alda wasn't interested in that woman's problems. She watched the woman enter her room before slipping out of the door.

Alda thanked Cora for her kindness and walked the two blocks to Mrs. Baxley's.

Uncle Larkin answered the back door.

"Alda, come in." He pulled her out of the scorching sun and into the cool of Mrs. Baxley's hall. "Why did you leave earlier? Are you upset about something?"

"I don't want to talk about it."

"I think you owe us an explanation. Cord asked me to find you, and you were gone. I told him, and he ran out the door with his guest yelling after him. Mrs. Baxley was quite upset no one stayed for dinner."

Who cared who did or didn't eat Mrs. Baxley's roast beef? "Cord was rude and so I left. As to the companion running after him, I can't help you there." Alda tugged at her uncle's sleeve. "Uncle Larkin, I need the money for the mules. I'll take it home, and I'll pay off the taxes like Ma and I planned. I want to leave today."

"I'm sorry, Alda. I can't do it."

"What do you mean you can't do it?"

"I can't give you the money; I don't have it."

"You said the mine gave you the money on Friday."

"Yup, they gave me the money, and I wired it to your pa."

"Noooo." Alda pressed her fingers to her temples; blood pounded against them. "Do you have any idea what you've done? Pa won't pay off the taxes. He'll come up with some ridiculous new scheme for improving the value of his stock." Mamma's plan was ruined. Alda's trip across the country — all the sacrifice — was a complete waste.

Alda's chest screwed down on her breaths like a Mason jar lid, and she rested her forehead against the wall.

"Listen — "

Alda had heard enough. She whirled around. "No, you listen! It never ends, Uncle Larkin. I'm telling you my father's delusion will not end until he's drug out of our home, kicking and screaming, and only then because our home belongs to someone else. My mother died trying to keep a roof over our heads, but she died in peace knowing we had a plan."

Uncle Larkin shrugged. "I couldn't, in good conscience, give you the money when I found out you had taken the mules without permission."

"So now what? I have no money to pay off the taxes. I have no money to go home."

Uncle Larkin put his hand in his pocket and pulled out several bills. "I can give you the money to get home."

"Why bother? It won't be my home for much longer. The county has been threatening a tax auction for months now." Where could she go?

"What about Cord? It's easy enough to see he's in love with you."

Alda snorted. "You're just as foolish as I was. I thought we were going to marry until he announced in Mrs. Baxley's parlor that we were not." She reached out and plucked the crumpled bills from Uncle Larkin's hand.

"So that's why you ran away," he said.

"Yes, that's why I ran away. And now that I have no reason to go home," she fanned the bills between them, "I'll use these to get to Oregon."

"Why don't you stay here, in Daggett? I'm sure we can find you some sort of work. Mrs. Baxley and her friends are always mentioning needing good help."

She couldn't stay. The town would always be a reminder of her foolishness and a reminder of Cord's unfaithfulness. "I met a couple when we traveled with the wagon train, the MacDarbys. The wife and I became good friends. She invited me to come and visit after they arrived in Oregon. They should arrive in a month or so. I'm sure I can find some work further north until they show up."

Uncle Larkin attempted to snatch the bills from Alda's hand, but she quickly hid them behind her back. "I can't let you take off for Oregon alone," he said.

"It's not even half as far as I've come already. You'll have to leave me in the Lord's hands like you did before. In a couple of weeks, I'll let you know where I am. Bridget was going to send you word when they arrived. If you pass on where they settled, I would appreciate it." Alda embraced her uncle in a hug. "I'll be going now, Uncle Larkin. You take care, all right?"

Uncle Larkin tightened his grip. "That man doesn't know what he's missing out on."

"Maybe that's just a proud uncle talking." Alda waved and slipped through the door.

She counted the bills Uncle Larkin had handed her as she crossed the yard. Between those and the money she had left from what Cord had given her, she could take the train to Oregon and wait it out until the MacDarbys arrived. Going to see Bridget, Grey, and the girls was a better idea than going home. Pa was probably still fuming about her taking the mules even if he'd settled down enough to let her out of jail. And if she wasn't at home, losing the farm to the county wouldn't hurt as much.

Bridget would enjoy Alda's company and her help with the twins. She could look for work while she stayed with the family.

Alda crossed the street and walked toward the livery stable. Cord or no Cord, there was no way she could leave town without saying goodbye to the mules. The smell of fresh hay greeted her as she walked through the open doors of the stable. Regardless, the mules would be happy to begin the couple of weeks in training they needed before they were hitched with another team to one of the enormous wagons.

Alda opened the gate to Bessie's pen and stepped inside. The mule nuzzled her neck and Alda folded herself around the mule's head.

"Bessie, I'm going to miss you girl. You've been nothing but a friend your whole life. I know you love to pull. You're going to like it here. Newt will take good care of you, and Uncle Larkin too." Alda slid her hand down the mule's back and slapped her belly. "You watch out for the others, all right?"

Alda left Bessie's stall and said goodbye to the mules one at a time. As she rubbed between Arthur's ears, she heard footsteps walking toward the barn door. Alda ducked her head. She didn't need any interruption to her farewell.

A gate creaked and a familiar voice said, "Hey, Bessie."

Of course, Cord would have to come to the barn. It would be too easy if Alda left town without hearing from or seeing him again. If she was quiet, maybe he would go his way without knowing she was there. Alda crouched down and leaned back into the rough corner boards of Arthur's stall.

"Where is she, Bessie? I know you'd tell me if you could."

Not if she knew what was good for her.

"Has she left town yet? I can't find her; I'm running out of places to look."

Why was he looking? So he could tell Alda face to face he had no intention of marrying her. *No. Thank. You.*

"I love her Bessie. I don't want to let her go."

But he didn't want to marry her either. The man was cruel. She pushed her fingernails into her palms and clamped her lips to keep from yelling out. *Move along, Cord, and let me get on with the business of leaving.*

"I want to make her my wife, Bessie."

Alda shot up from her corner in Arthur's stall. "You'd

lie to a mule?"

Cord turned, and his hand stopped midway on its path down Bessie's back. "Alda? You're still here?" He closed his eyes and lifted his face to the ceiling. "Thank You, Lord," he murmured.

"Not for long. It's one thing to take advantage of me." Alda raised her finger to point at Cord over the rail. "But I will not permit you to manipulate my mule." She wrenched the gate open and stalked down the alley. Planting her feet in the dirt and jamming her hands on her hips as she faced Cord. "Get away from Bessie."

Cord raised his palms in a pleading gesture and took one step back from the mule. "Alda, I'm sorry." He lowered his tone. "I understand why you're upset. If you'll let me ex — "

"Explain what? Did you not tell your beautiful friend we were not getting married?"

"No, I didn't — "

Alda stamped her foot. "I heard you with my own ears!"

"All right, I said that, but — "

Alda tromped over and dug her boots into the hay within inches of Cord's. The man had no shame. "Get away from my mule," she ground out between her teeth.

"She's my sister. Victoria's my sister."

Alda stared at Cord. Did she just hear him right? "The woman in the parlor was your sister?"

"Yes, I didn't get a chance to introduce you. My father had me followed, and when Hayden finally caught up with me, he sent my sister."

"So it was your sister you told we weren't getting married."

"I'm sorry I hurt you."

"It's what men do, isn't it? Fathers, friends…" Alda bit her bottom lip to keep it from quivering. She watched as Cord's Adam's apple rose and then fell.

"Before I say anything else, I have to tell you something."

Tell her what? She wasn't good enough for his family and —

"Your father didn't have a change of heart."

Her pa? What did he have to do with this? "What do you mean?"

"I should have told you before. Your pa didn't change his mind about accusing you. I bought the mules from him so he would withdraw the charges."

"How?"

"When the sheriff in Cheyenne told me you were in prison, I took the train to your farm and talked to your pa. He agreed to sell me the mules."

"If I know Pa, they didn't come cheap."

"I don't want to keep anything from you, Alda. I paid him three thousand dollars."

"Well, I guess the deal my father had been waiting for his whole life finally showed up. Uncle Larkin sent him the money from the mine, too." A single tear ran from the corner of Alda's eye. "If you hadn't shown up, my pa was going to leave me in jail, wasn't he?"

Cord reached over and wiped the tear with his thumb. "Probably."

Oregon sounded even better now. "I need to go." She turned to leave Bessie's stall.

"There's more."

Alda turned back to face Cord. "More? Don't you think that's enough, Cord?"

"I paid him another three thousand dollars to sign the paper for your release."

What was he saying? Her father had sold her like she was livestock. Alda closed her eyes to quell the dizziness. She needed to get out of the barn and breathe in some fresh air — fast. Alda took a step forward.

Cord's arms came around her shoulders.

"Don't touch me," she said, batting him away. "So my pa doesn't love me, and you paid for me. What a waste of your money!"

"I wanted you out of jail. Your pa took advantage of me, but I would do it again. I would give everything I have to be with you."

Alda dropped her head to stare at the ground. "But not marry me," she whispered.

"This is the last place I imagined I would ever do this." Cord got down on one knee in the muck of the stall and reached out to hold Alda's left hand. "Miss Alda Lealand, would you do me the honor of becoming my wife? I don't have the ring with me, and there's not much chance of finding it, seeing as it's in the pass west of Laramie, but I can buy a new one. Just give me some time to recover from some recent financial losses."

Cord's smile held the promise of a lifetime together — loving each other and loving the Lord. "I will," she said. "I will marry you!" She leaned forward to press her lips against his.

Epilogue

Ding, dong, ding, dong. The bells of St. Mary's Memorial Presbyterian rang out as Cord and Alda turned at the altar and faced the church full of wedding guests.

Cord looked down at Alda and smiled, his eyes filled with the love they felt for one another, a love which had blossomed and grown since arriving in Marysville a month ago. Alda's heart swelled as she looked up at her new husband.

The local church ladies had welcomed Alda like the motherless girl she was, and helped her plan the special day. They'd filled the church with lavish arrangements of white hydrangeas, red roses, and ivy. Cord had asked for red roses, a reminder of her beautiful long hair. Alda reached up to smooth the short curls at the nape of her neck.

She carried a miniature version of the church arrangements in a bouquet laced with Cord's grandmother's white pearls. Victoria had given them to Alda a couple of days before. An olive branch of sorts from Cord's father and mother who couldn't attend the service. Victoria had also reminded Cord of his promise to visit the home place before the year's end. Perhaps it would become part of their honeymoon. Cord's new job as Sheriff of Marysville wouldn't allow for more than a weekend at a country inn after today's nuptials.

Alda looked down at her bouquet — perfect against the

white of her wedding dress. Ellen, a local dressmaker, had sown a dress fit for any magazine page. The white satin brocade folded and tucked into a large bustle trimmed with white lace and looped with a wide white ribbon. The front panel of the dress ran in pleats of white brocade and white velvet. Thanks to Ellen, Alda was dressed like a princess.

Ruby and Pearl scampered down the aisle in white satin dresses trimmed with the same lace. Cord had sent money for the family to attend the wedding. Bridget and the girls arrived a week ago to help out with all the final arrangements. Alda had appreciated the assistance, and Bridget's musical laughter made their tasks easier. Grey was busy working on their new sheep ranch outside of Dayville, Oregon, and couldn't attend.

Alda's father and his new wife did not attend either. Cord had told Alda about her father's hasty marriage when they left the barn after Cord's proposal. Every day, the thought of the marriage twisted in Alda's stomach. Her mamma deserved better and forgiveness of her father was proving difficult.

The shame of the marriage probably wasn't what kept Alda's pa away from her wedding, though. By rights, he should be giving the money from the mine to Cord. The animals weren't even her pa's when her uncle had sent him the payment. Pa knew Alda would take him to task over the money if he showed his face. And she just might ask him why he was willing to sell his only daughter when he had such a hard time selling his mules. It was one of the few things her pa had done right even if he hadn't meant to.

"So, Mrs. Alda Sweet, are you ready?" Cord leaned over and whispered in her ear.

Alda looked up, looped her arm through his, and gave him her best smile. She couldn't be more ready to share her life with Cord — learning more about him and the God who would be the center of their marriage. Her future looked bright knowing they'd both promised her an everlasting love.

Her mamma would've been so proud of Alda's decision to love the Lord and to marry someone who loved Him just as much as she did. "I'm ready," she whispered back.

Cord drew Alda down the church aisle, following the girls, and out onto the wide steps beyond the church's heavy, double doors. Rice, thrown by their excited guests, hit and bounced off their clothing. Alda lifted her hand to shield her eyes from some of the overzealous pellets.

Her breath caught. Across the yard, with an enormous crimson bow tied around her neck, stood a mule, the lead held fast by Rosie's oldest daughter Emma. Rosie and her family had rented a small farm outside of Marysville after Cord had found her work cleaning and providing meals for the prisoners at the sheriff's office.

Alda's hand tightened on Cord's bicep. "Cord, is that who I think it is?"

He placed his hand on hers. "Your wedding gift, my love."

Alda tossed her bouquet, scrunched the skirt of her dress in both hands, then sprinted down the stairs and past the surprised guests to … Bessie.

The End

Thanks for reading!

To connect with me visit my website at:

www.lisajflickinger.com

If you sign up for my quarterly newsletter, I will keep you informed about upcoming novels!

My other books available on the website or on Amazon:

All That Glitters

Pushed by the desire to see the family reunited before her father's death, Vivian Connor chases her errant sister, Ginny, to the far north during the gold rush. Heartbreak and danger plague her journey across the country to a world plum crazy over gold. Can Vivian convince Ginny to forgive herself and return home? Will Vivian find love in the process?

Ella

Ella Goodwin, abandoned by her father and abused by her stepsister, seeks to make sense of her new life as a prisoner in her Washington D.C. home. By secretly designing and sewing a magnificent gown, she plans to attend the grand ball and meet Thomas Bailey, a disgraced Foreign Service Officer and her only hope for rescue. Will Ella's Prince Charming unravel the mystery and learn the true identity of the beautiful woman who has captured his heart?

Ella

Chapter One

Washington D.C. 1870

Ella pulled the long sliver from her finger, squeezed her eyes at the sight of the crimson droplet, and popped the digit into her mouth. Iron flowed across her tongue.

The wide, oak planks of the parlor should've been as smooth as a baby's bottom by now. It was her mother's design, the pretty, two story, brick house with its symmetrical windows and tall, white columns and it was older than Ella – who would be nineteen years in one month. Three times alone since Monday, Ella's bruised shins had carried her around the vestibule, the guest parlor, and the music room. When her stepsister Dru couldn't come up with another, floor scrubbing with a stiff brush and lye soap was Ella's assigned task. Dru must have been busy today, but at least Ella escaped the more tedious and demeaning chores.

Ella's eyelids snapped up at the clatter of the screen door. Dru giggled and a male voice chuckled in response. Had her stepsister found a new love so soon? Last week she'd been leading George, Ella's oldest friend, around by the nose.

Two figures stepped to the doorway of the parlor.

It *was* George. Ella pulled her finger from her mouth and her cheeks warmed at the resounding "slurp". She dropped her head and tucked her finger into the folds of her dingy homespun skirt.

Why was he chuckling in such an obnoxious, metered tone? The George Ella loved would clutch his stomach with both hands as sweaty, blond curls bounced around his chin and beg her to stop making him laugh.

They'd spent most of their childhood afternoons in the narrow thicket between the two homes building makeshift castles and barricades for holding off the enemy. He'd promised to protect Ella forever; it wasn't the only promise George had broken.

Dru lifted a gloved hand and fixed her hateful green eyes on Ella. "Dear ... sweet... Ella," she said, and emphasized each word by plucking the glove off her fingers one at a time.

"Yes, Dru?"

"I see you're scrubbing the floor again." Her glance landed on the wooden bucket sitting a few feet away.

Of course Ella was scrubbing the floor; Mother Adeline had said it was what Dru wanted.

"I'm assuming this means mother neglected to give you

my list of chores for today." Dru pulled the glove off her other hand and beat the silky pair against the peach taffeta of her skirt.

So Dru had left a list – not surprising. Ella glanced up at George. The skin above his starched, linen collar was turning a soft shade of pink. She reached up and tucked several wayward, white-blond strands of hair up into her cap.

George coughed and averted his gaze.

Tears prickled behind Ella's eyes, but she would not let them fall, not when the others could watch. "I'll finish the scrubbing and then look for your list."

"I don't think the day is long enough. We have some special occasions coming up and I need to make sure everything is perfect. I'll fetch the list and you can begin immediately. Mother!"

Ella flinched at the nasal screech. What did Dru mean by "she needed to make sure everything is perfect"? Were the girls thinking of entertaining? They hadn't until now. It would come as a welcome distraction even if Ella had to polish the silver, clean the windows, launder the curtains, and do whatever else Dru could come up with.

"Come along, George." Dru swished by Ella, and as she passed the cleaning bucket Dru's boot shot out to catch it on its side and tip it over. A murky puddle spread across the floor boards and began to disappear between the cracks.

George bent to right the bucket; as his hand grasped its rim, Ella reached out to do the same. Her hand closed over his. George flashed an angry look and uttered a foul word under his breath while jerking his hand back.

Was Ella that repulsive to him now?

George straightened and scurried after Dru whose bustle bounced with vigor as they trotted through the archway to the dining room.

Ella stood the bucket upright and used a rag to sop up the remaining water before she dropped to her knees and resumed her scrubbing.

How could George be so faithless? Why didn't he care that she was being kept like a prisoner in her own home?

And where was the Lord in all this? She'd been faithful to God her whole life. She read her Bible, prayed every day, and attended Pastor Dartley's services unfailingly. Her mother had always promised a pious life meant the Lord would protect you. *Forsake me not, O Lord: O my God, be not far from me.*

Dru took great delight in devising evil plots to make her suffer. Egbertha, for the most part, kept to herself and didn't interfere. Their mother Adeline's energies ran only to finding the best outfit for the day's weather. And with a dressing room full of new clothes, it took until early afternoon to be outfitted as woman of her new station.

Mother Adeline wasn't mean like Dru though. Silly, inept, and easily manipulated, but Ella's father, Isaac Goodwin, had married Adeline for her beauty. Beauty she still carried in her delicate shoulders and porcelain features, much like the doll now hidden upstairs in an old musty trunk in Ella's attic bedroom.

Ella's father had brought the doll home from one of his postings abroad when Ella was a small child. Egbertha had been the first to remark on the similarity between the doll's wide, blue eyes, rosy cheeks, and sweet, Cupid's bow mouth and their own mother's face. After Egbertha had done so, her lips had curled into their telltale smirk and her eyes had filled with the mocking laughter she liked to bestow on Ella when Egbertha finally emerged from her room. The remark was almost enough to make Ella lift the china doll above her head, drop it to the floor, and let it break into a hundred pieces, but she hadn't given Egbertha the satisfaction.

Ella's father had left with only a half-day' notice two months after marrying Mother Adeline and only three months after Ella's mother's death. A foreign minister had been recalled from the office in Bombay. Although retired her father had agreed to cover the post for a few months, no longer than a year, until a suitable replacement could be found or manufactured.

Isaac had no idea Adeline had moved her daughters into the home shortly after he left for Bombay. In fact, he had no idea Adeline even had daughters of her own, she'd never told him. Because of his hasty marriage to a woman he hardly knew, Ella suffered daily.

He'd been gone five months without sending Ella a single reply to all the letters she had written him detailing the extent of Dru's cruelty and Mother Adeline's allowing it. Ella glanced through the doorway toward the empty silver tray on the hall table. Perhaps today would be the day she would finally have word.

"Ella, darling." Adeline entered through the dining room doorway Dru and George trailing behind her. She tipped her pretty head and her brows furrowed into a tiny vee.

Ella almost blurted out Egbertha's daily warning. "Mother, relax your face or you'll ruin your looks." Which was always followed with Egbertha's whispered "and we all know it's all you've got" behind a polite hand.

"Ella, why is your dress sopping wet?" Mother Adeline asked.

Ella glanced at the wet stains in the folds around her knees and then glanced over Mother Adeline's shoulder toward Dru. "The buck –"

"The silly girl spilled the cleaning bucket again. It's the third time in as many weeks, Mother. I guess she needs more practice. Here, let me help you up." Dru brushed by her mother and gripped Ella above the elbow digging her fingernails into the flesh on the inside of Ella's arm.

Ella didn't need the warning. Of course she wouldn't tell Mother Adeline Dru had kicked the bucket over. There was no way to prove it. She couldn't rely on George to side with her and telling would only bring further wrath from Dru in the future.

Ella tugged her arm from Dru's grasp and formed a tight knot with her hands to keep from lashing out. A steady drip, drip hit the floorboards from the hem of her skirt.

"I must be going," George said as he nodded curtly at Mother Adeline and then Dru.

Please do. His presence made Ella's humiliation so much more complete.

"George, aren't you forgetting something?" Dru spoke to his back as he retreated through the vestibule doorway.

He turned to face them and Dru tapped the side of her cheek with a single finger. George coughed twice before returning to plant a single, swift kiss where Dru's finger had pointed.

Ella couldn't help the gasp which escaped her chest.

Dru's plump lips turned up into a tight smile and she

fluttered her eyelashes as George left the parlor.

Why was George behaving like some sort of trained dog?

"Ella, would you please go and change your skirt?" Mother Adeline asked.

"But, Mother, we were going to talk about my list."

"Dru, you can see the girl is soaking wet." Mother Adeline lifted her hands, palms up, and fluttered them. "Hurry now, Ella, up to your room quickly. You will find us in the music room when you return."

Ella trudged up the flight of stairs at the back of the front hall one leaden foot after another. Dru's insistence that Ella rise with the roosters made for a long day and further cruelty as the others didn't awake until mid-morning. Her eyelids drooped momentarily, blurring the delicate roses on the carpet runner; Ella shook her head and took a deep breath to wake herself.

Why wasn't George doing anything about her situation? Surely he couldn't be blinded by love for Dru regardless of their display in the parlor. The thought was preposterous. The mother's looks had definitely not passed down to either girl.

Dru's sturdy frame was topped by a broad head covered in frizzy, black hair. Her cheeks were plump and often covered by the sheen of overexertion. Not from work — to be sure. Her full lips pursed in a pout at the slightest provocation and her upturned nose spent most of its time in the air.

So if it wasn't her looks that held him, what was it?

"There you are." As Ella reached the top stair, the languid voice spoke from the darkness of Egbertha's bedroom.

Egbertha had said earlier she would be running errands in the afternoon.

"Come here."

Ella stopped outside the bedroom door. "I'm to change my clothes and return to the music room straightaway."

"I said come here."

Ella put her hand to the ornate, walnut door and applied pressure slowly. If Egbertha was having one of her headaches even how the door opened would make her vomit.

The room was warm. Ella wrinkled her nose at the scent of lavender cloaking old sweat.

Egbertha lay across the large, feather bed, Ella's former bed, with one arm shielding her eyes. "Did you have to stomp up the stairs like an elephant when you know I have a headache?"

Ella hadn't stomped, neither did she know Egbertha had a headache, but there was no point arguing with her at the best of times, let alone when she was in pain. "I'm sorry, can I get you something?"

Egbertha lifted her arm to expose one eye and scowled. "Of course you can get me something. No one else seems to care."

Egbertha's lean torso and bony limbs were a severe contrast to her sister's plumpness. Her narrow face and small, dark eyes reminded Ella of the voles the gardener trapped after they munched his carrots. And the large, lumpy wart in the middle of one cheek did nothing to add to her features.

"What would you like? A glass of water, a cool cloth for

your forehead, both?"

"My powders are in the drawer of mother's beside table. Bring me some."

"But your mother said I wasn't —"

"Bring me some," Egbertha ground out between her misshapen teeth.

Ella scuttled out of the room and two doors down to her father and Mother Adeline's bedroom. After they'd married, it was the only room Ella's father had allowed his new wife to redecorate and only after Adeline had whined incessantly for a week.

How sad he had given in. The hired decorator suggested bold contrasts and the room had become a mish mash of oranges, blues, and greens. From the ornately patterned, owl wallpaper to the intricate, Turkish rug, Ella's gaze darted around like it had nowhere to land.

She crossed the room to the bedside table and looked over her shoulder. Ella wasn't allowed in the room; Adeline would be furious if she caught her. Ella opened the top drawer of the table too far and stooped to catch it. As she did so, a packet of letters appeared in the gap behind the drawer.

Ella put the drawer on the carpet and reached for the packet. It held ten letters tied in a white ribbon. She flipped through them; they were all dated in the last five months, the address written in a familiar scrawl – her own. Her stomach clenched into a tight ball. That's why her father hadn't replied to her letters. Adeline hadn't posted them. Isaac had no idea he'd left his daughter in the hands of such cruel taskmasters. Ella swallowed the bitter taste in her mouth. There would be no help coming from her father.

Ella placed the letters in their hiding spot and snatched the small brown bottle labeled Dover's Powders from the drawer before sliding it back into the table. She returned to Egbertha's room where she lay exactly as Ella had left her. "How many would you like?"

"Two, I need at least two," Egbertha's voice trembled.

"Two then, and no more. Remember last time when you took three? You were violently ill." Ella pulled the cork and upturned the bottle until two white tablets rolled into her palm. Extending her hand to Egbertha, she said, "I'll fetch you a glass of water."

Egbertha sat up and her hand snaked out to take the tablets from Ella's palm. She stuck them in her mouth and chewed vigorously. "I don't need any water; I'll be fine in a moment."

"You know your mother will be angry if she finds some missing."

"I'll find a way to replace them. Mother needs to mind her own affairs." Egbertha smoothed the ruffles of her blue silk sleeves before planting her dark gaze on Ella. "And so do you. You won't mention a single word of this to anyone if you know what's good for you."

What would be good for Ella would be to leave this house — a house full of terrible secrets.

"Ella! Where are you?" Dru called up the stairway.

Ella ran from Egbertha's room. "I'll be down in a moment," she said over her shoulder as she raced down the hall and up the narrow attic steps. The girls had thought supplanting Ella from her beautiful room on the second story to the long, narrow room under the eaves would be a punishment. It was a godsend. The others didn't bother to navigate the narrow stairway, and it had become her sanctuary. Ella had tucked most of the stored items along the far wall in a tidy stack leaving lots of room for three tables and two dressmaker's forms she'd found amongst the clutter. Several bolts of fabric rested on one of the tables, several sketches and a hand drawn pattern on the other.

Ella crossed to the other end of the room where a narrow cot and a bulky wardrobe formed her sleeping quarters. After removing the sopping skirt, she grabbed another drab one from the wardrobe to replace it. If she took much longer, Dru might decide to come and find her and that would spoil everything.

78219831R00137

Made in the USA
Columbia, SC
13 October 2017